Chatterhat

Matt Ingwalson
© 2021

ISBN 978-0-578-87857-7

Table of Contents

Chapter 1
The Story of the Magic Frog

My favorite joke is:

"The other day, I went out golfing. First one on the course, beautiful day, early, really early, dawn's coming up. There's dew on the grass, nobody else in sight.

"I step up to the first tee. Par four, little dogleg going off to the right, so I tee up my ball and pull out my three wood. And from somewhere down on the ground I hear a tiny voice say, 'Ribbit. Two iron.' I look down and there on the very edge of the tee box, there's a little green frog looking back at me.

"I didn't know what to do so I said, 'What?' And again, the frog said, 'Ribbit. Two iron.' I'm like, two iron on a par four? Makes no sense, right? I say it though, 'Two iron?' Like, what am I doing, I'm talking to a frog?

"He says, 'Ribbit.'

"I swear, it was like I was hypnotized. I slid my three wood back into my bag, took out my two iron, didn't settle in or nothing, just hacked at it. Bang. Knocked it two inches from the cup."

Sometimes at this point in the joke, I wave two fingers in a V in the air and say again, "Two inches."

Then, "I looked down at this frog and said something articulate like, 'How?'

"Frog replies, 'Ribbit. Magic frog.'

"And again, I'm like, 'What?' Like, magic frog, right?

"Frog just looks up at me.

"OK, so I pick that magic frog up, put him right on top of my bag, carry him with me. We get to the next tee, he says, 'Ribbit. Driver.' I use my driver. Hole in one. Swear. I am not a good golfer, this was the first hole in one I had had ever in my entire life.

"This went on all day. I think I shot, like, a fifty-nine. Like, half what I shoot.

"So I put that magic frog in a duffel bag, head straight to the airport, buy a ticket on the next plane to Las Vegas. And when I get there, I walk right into Caesar's Palace and say, 'Magic Frog, what should I do?'

"And he goes, 'Ribbit. Roulette.' I walk up to the nearest roulette table and the frog just speaks out of nowhere. 'Ribbit. Eight.'

"And I do it. I go for it. All in. I put it all on eight. Not just all my golf money. Everything. My mortgage, everything in my savings account, I throw my watch on there. All of it. The croupier is just shaking his head, people start walking up, saying, what is this guy doing? My heart just, like, pounding, what the hell was I doing?

"Croupier guy throws the ball and it starts going round and around. Everybody is holding their breath. The wheel starts to slow, the ball starts bouncing, bouncing. Finally, settles right in. Eight.

"Oh my god. Lights start ringing. There was, like, a siren, I think. Everyone slapping me on my back and shaking my hand. I'm just an average guy, suddenly I'm a millionaire.

"Pit boss comes by to congratulate me, take a picture, and he comps me a suite. A suite at Caesars. And not just any suite, this thing was gorgeous. All the way up near the top floor. Personal bar stocked with, like, fancy vodkas and wine. Picture windows, I could see all of the Strip out there, winking at me. I'm King Of The Strip. El Capo De Las Vegas. And right in the center of this room, there's a big heart-shaped bed with gold satin sheets on it.

"So I took that magic frog out of my bag, place it on my bed, and say to it, 'Magic frog, thank you. You have made me rich and happy beyond my wildest dreams. How can I ever repay you?'

"And the frog goes, 'Ribbit. Kiss me.'

"I say, 'Kiss you?'

"And the frog says again, 'Ribbit. Kiss me.'

"Well, what could I do? I mean, I owed everything to that frog. What's one little kiss? So I take a deep breath and lean down and kiss the frog right on the top of its head. And immediately, whoosh, there was a thunderclap and a big poof of smoke! And as it clears I see the frog has changed and now, in its place, there's this beautiful girl. Totally naked. Lying right in the middle of my bed.

"And that, Your Honor, is how she got into my room

last night."

I have been telling that joke for, like, 10 years.

Sometimes I change details. Like, I'll throw in a side bet with another golfer, which the protagonist wins and that's what inspires him to go to Vegas.

Or I mention or not-mention the name of the casino. Or change the destination, one time it's Atlantic City, another it is Monte Carlo. Vegas works best. I think that's because everyone already has a picture of Vegas in their heads, so they don't leave my story for a second trying to remember where Monte Carlo is or imagining what Atlantic City looks like.

In the summer, I often mention the story starts "yesterday morning." But in the winter, I have to skip that part and just begin with, "So I'm out golfing..."

Occasionally I experiment with more meaningful details, like whether or not to mention the age of the girl. I've found it's best to just leave it out. If she's like 18 or 25 or 30, people get distracted. Maybe they start to wonder why I'm being so specific? Or how my protagonist could have known what her age was anyway? Or maybe it's one detail too many, and suddenly they're trying to imagine what she looked like? On the other hand, if she's underage, like 16, the joke is DOA. You can actually see the audience tuck in their chins, like they're physically gauging whether they should call child protective services on me. This is especially true if the person I'm telling the joke to is a parent.

Anyway, the reason I love this joke isn't that it's so, so funny. (Although over time and with a bunch of practice, I've learned to tell it so it always gets a laugh.) And it's not that it illustrates the elements of clear storytelling. (Although it includes an inciting incident, three distinct acts, a climax, a character arc, repetition, allusion, a protagonist, a phantom antagonist, etc.)

No, the real reason I love The Story of the Magic Frog is that it doesn't behave like other jokes. There's no punchline. There's only a calculation. A plan. A twist. A turn of the screw.

Throughout the joke, listeners assume they're passive observers waiting for a laugh. This perception is encouraged by familiar elements like a talking frog, and reinforced by the repetition of a silly word.

Ribbit.

But The Story of the Magic Frog doesn't work like a conventional joke at all. At the very last possible moment, listeners find they are, in fact, active participants. They are a character in my joke. They are my accomplice. And they laugh because of the way the punchline forces them to readjust their perception not just of the unlikely story, but of their own complicity in it.

Sometimes the joke's on you. And other times, you're the joke.

Chapter 2
Invisibility

It looked like there was a blue and yellow anaconda with a blue and yellow fleur de lis camouflage wrapping itself around the woman's neck and pulling her into its hideously large face. There wasn't, of course. The anaconda was actually a neck pillow. The hideously large face was real though. It belonged to her husband. At least, I hoped it was her husband and not just the guy she happened to be sitting next to on the 888x.

Their two round faces were perfect O's and connected at that one small spot, their lips, they made the shape of an hourglass on its side, an infinity loop that hovered in the air as I watched them kiss from one row behind, across an empty seat.

Nobody likes being around me much anymore. For this, I have The Evidence of the Empty Seat. The seat next to me on the bus is always empty and I don't know why, or how every stranger who boards the bus knows to avoid me.

I don't take up much room. I'm always showered, inoffensively dressed. I'm also reasonably skinny, so it's not like my gut is lava-flowing over the armrest.

For a while I thought maybe I carried with me a smell I'd grown so used to living with that I couldn't smell it anymore. I tried several things to combat this possibly nonexistent smell including showering twice a day; going to hot yoga instead of playing basketball or whatever; several different deodorants, colognes and Eau Fraiches; various mouthwashes, with active ingredients including cetylpyridinium chloride, alcohol and essential oils; drinking ungodly amounts of water; and chewing gum on my way to the bus stop. None of this seemed to make much of a difference. I didn't really think I smelled anyway, but I didn't have anybody to ask and I wanted to be sure.

I tried scooting farther and farther over in my seat, far enough I was practically glued to the window, a part of the bus itself. Still, people would get on the bus one by one and slide in next to anyone not me. The old woman who kept coughing a dense wet cough without even trying to cover her mouth. The fat man who took the window seat and when he got up his sweat left a moisture stain on the window. The girl who was wearing a miniskirt but who was clearly so uncomfortable in it only some sort of pervert would sit next to her and make her feel even more uncomfortable, forcing her to touch thighs with a stranger like that. And yet the seat next to me remained empty, stop after stop, day after day.

After almost a year of trying to be invisible, I feared perhaps I had succeeded.

The woman with the anaconda neck pillow was doing one of those laughs as she got inhaled by her husband's face, a laugh that seemed endearing and unique when you were dating but which you knew post-marriage would drive you insane. A parrot mimicking a fire alarm. Still, she was sitting next to someone, someone who liked her enough to sit by her and kiss her on the mouth.

I got to the end of the line, got off, and waited six and a half minutes for the next 888x to come around and take me back home. I wasn't going anywhere, just killing time experimenting with various things, examining The Evidence of the Empty Seat.

Perhaps, I thought as I rode back home, perhaps I ought to make an effort. Like after eleven months of living in Winegrove, my neighborhood, I ought to throw myself a housewarming party and see if the neighbors liked me. Maybe they would, if they met me. I'd probably be infinitely more likeable if they were all drinking wine in my kitchen. At least I wouldn't be invisible. Or would I? That would be awful, to have people over and then they ignore you. If they came over and ignored you, it'd be really awful.

I don't lie to people about my name per se, but those who know me now know me as Bob, whereas those who used to know me knew me as Rob and that little change, it is amazing how much difference it makes.

My real name, obviously, is Robert.

I used to have a ton of t-shirts. Like, a ton. Many of these were concert t-shirts, usually bought on a tour, which means they had a date on them. And then I had many sports t-shirts, which also were pretty recognizable, at least because they had a city name on them which, geographically, located me. And then sports teams often change their insignia as well, which means each t-shirt had a date attached to it, even if non-sports fans didn't recognize that date, necessarily.

I threw all these t-shirts out, which was painful but I did it to prevent me from wearing them.

The unfortunate thing, though, is that sports and concerts and even names are signifiers. They tell people you are part of the tribe that likes a specific team or band, or just a given genre of sport or music in general, one which maybe you played at a real high school in a real town. These signifiers then engender conversation and conversation tends to enable likability as long as you don't royally mess it up. So when I threw away my t-shirts, I threw away all my tribal signifiers and thus lost an easy conversational gambit.

What tees I have now are all just plain and white, except for my Moo Cow milk delivery shirt, which I am required to wear by Moo Cow company code and which has a cow on it because milk, get it?

I started buying sneakers after I threw out my tees, and I have a lot of them. I spend way too much time shopping for sneakers online. I even have an app that I prowl around on so I don't get scammed on Webworld. I started playing basketball at the courts in my hood purely because I owned three pairs of basketball sneakers, and it made me feel like a fraud to own them and not even be able to dribble a basketball.

As soon as I installed said app, I started getting served ads for things related to sneakers in specific and athleisure wear in general. Dismissing these ads takes a flick of the thumb, a fraction of a second. But there seem to be a lot of them and dismissing them all the time became a game almost unto itself, one which I seemed to have to play for quite awhile every single day.

But time is relative when you don't have a job. Except the milk delivery thing, which is a very part-time job, which has the side benefits of being solitary and quiet. I have a pretty good amount of time on my hands, is my point. But I don't have a lot of shirt options.

So when I get out of my house and down the sidewalk and up the twisty sidewalk of my neighbor's and ring the doorbell, I am wearing a white t-shirt and sneakers. My neighbor is wearing a polo shirt with the logo of the state justice department on it and he's wearing it with cargo shorts. He says Bob when he greets me, which is a total shock to me as I don't know his name at all. I feel terribly embarrassed and try to cover up for this with a jocularity so forced it probably feels as inauthentic to him as it does to me.

"Hey, long time no see."

"Lawn's looking good. My wife asked, 'What's the secret to Bob's lawn?'"

I pay a service to do this, make my lawn look good. Sometimes I even sit in my window and watch them mow my lawn. They seem to be half white college kids and half Hispanic seniors. The crew never seems to talk to each other much. Maybe there is a language barrier? That same crew or at least that same company then prunes my bushes and fertilizes (or whatever) my flowers, which are of a yellow and purple sort I can't name beyond that yellowness and purpleness. At one point, I decided I should take over and for two seconds even took pride in how much I was learning about lawn care. But I secretly hate it and only have a lawn at all because of a sense of obligation, a need not to be that house that everyone in the neighborhood walks by and secretly resents. So I never actually took over. I let the lawn company do it. And it is on their behalf that I graciously and genuinely accept this compliment from, from... damnit. From this neighbor human.

"Thanks. So I've been working on the house. The inside I mean, not the outside," I stumble. I prepared this story and I am bungling it already, but I plow through. I laugh for no real reason and show him open palms, which makes people like you more and makes them think you have nothing to hide, according to some videos I watched on Webworld on the topic of being liked more. "And I was thinking since I have been here, in the neighborhood I bit, a bit, I mean... I was thinking I'd see if some of the folks wanted to come over for a housewarming party."

"Well, sure," he says.

"Sure, that's great," I say, taken aback by how well this conversation is going despite my fumbling. "I was thinking a week from Saturday?"

"Is this kids? Or adults only? Not one of Dana's parties, right?" my next door neighbor asks. He laughs a bit, like this is an inside joke, but unfortunately I am not on the inside, and in fact don't even know who Dana is, and also I am panicking a bit because I hadn't predicted the kid question in any way, shape or form. I know, of course, that many people in my neighborhood, most of whom are older than me but not drastically so, have kids. I see them riding Big Wheels in their cul de sacs and playing football in their lawns. But do these kids come to adult parties?

I say, "You know, I was going to just see. If people want to bring kids, I have a TV in the basement, they can hang. Unless, if they're too young…"

"Tell you what, Bob, I'll ask Mindy. Maybe they're getting old enough we can leave 'em here. It's right next door." He leans into me. "You know, up to me, I think they're old enough. But Mindy?"

Quick mental note: this neighbor's wife's name is Mindy. We confirm that some iteration of their family is coming over a week from Saturday.

After he closes the door I walk back home and make a note of this on a little piece of paper. I fold up the little piece of paper and put it in my pocket so I can write down any other neighbors' names I happen to learn.

Anyway, a scene either exactly like this or similar to this plays itself out at the next three houses. Then I cross the street and visit six houses going back the other way, and then I cross the street again and hit the three houses on the other side of me. In total, in 20 minutes, I had three men and four women talk to me. Also two kids whose parents weren't home.

At three houses no one answered, but at one of them, I swear I saw movement behind the curtains as I walked away, back down the sidewalk.

Chapter 3
Submission

Around seven o' clock two Saturday nights later, I'd started to get worried that no one was going to come to my party. I'd told people they could start dropping by around seven, which seemed like a safe time. But maybe it wasn't because no one had shown up.

But by 11 o' clock I was worrying, what if these people never left? There were adults in the kitchen, adults doing shots, like real adults with kids who were sleeping in my basement, the kids' adults doing crazy toxic shots like Alabama Slammers and Apocalypse Nows and Poudre Canyon Drop Offs.

But at midnight, everybody turned into pumpkins. Like an alarm had gone off, they all filed down into my basement and lifted up the sleeping bags containing, I hoped, their sleeping kids and stumbled away and, I assumed, home. Which was good because I was starting to worry about how I was going to get to work if they didn't leave.

Now, just a couple hours later, I'm standing on a sidewalk having a friendly and surprisingly articulate conversation with a guy wearing a woman's latex miniskirt around his waist and a leash around his neck. The leash is made from pink leather and silvery chain, and it indefinitely attaches him to the patio of Moo Cow Farms Milk Delivery headquarters.

The guy's name is John, because of course it is, and he is explaining that he can't remove his leash until his mistress comes to "collect her pet." He speaks in the honest, deep voice you'd expect of a mustachioed, slightly-overweight, forty-year-old guy.

"For people who live the BSD&M lifestyle, humiliation is an important part of who we are," he tells me.

"I get that," I say. "I do. But by doing this here in public, you've made me part of your lifestyle."

I point toward the window of Moo Cow. In that little amber square, we can see the thin teenage counter receptionist who somehow works here almost every night, even during the school year. I'd always assumed maybe she was one of the owner's kids, but maybe she's a runaway. I'd never asked, because knowing people's backstories is not a thing I'm sure I want to do.

She, the receptionist, is staring out at us, chin in her palm, face dark with either eyeshadow or actual shadows.

"See that girl?" I point. "You've made her part of your lifestyle. All the people walking in to my work, none of us want to be a part of your act here."

"It's not an act."

"Sorry, that was a bad choice of words. But, like, your lifestyle, none of us want to be part of it."

"But without you all, there's no one to be humiliated in front of. Look, my sexuality isn't something I can change."

"But this is a milk delivery business. Shouldn't you have been chained up in front of a porn store downtown in Aspenroot or something?"

"I don't ask my mistress these questions."

"But this is the suburbs. We are definitely not living in your, like, world. We are not your target audience."

"Well, if any of you needed me to do anything so you could express your sexuality, I'd be glad to trade."

"Dude? Seriously, nobody wants to trade. Everyone here just thinks you're silly." I pause. "Shoot, that just made it even better for you, right? Because I insulted you?"

"Nah, don't worry about it. You've kind of killed the mood."

I'm searching for a solution for him, and I don't know why. I need to leave on my route soon. "Couldn't you just be humiliated in front of your mistress person? That's who, like, you worship, right?"

"We do that too. Last weekend she made me drink her urine from a dog bowl."

"OK, see, that's what I'm talking about. Now I know that. I didn't want to know that, but now I do. So you're humiliating me, and isn't that the opposite of what you're trying to do here?"

The guy's eyes get wide and he considers. "Yeah, yeah, it's a good point."

I feel relieved. "Cool, do you have, like, clothes somewhere?"

"No, my mistress holds my clothes until my humiliation is over."

"Dude, John, your humiliation is totally over. It is so over." I put my hands casually into my pockets and look around. There are a few people watching from streetside. Over our counter receptionist's shoulder, there are a couple new heads bobbing, necks craning, Moo Cow employees trying to see just what the heck is happening. Which is, in my opinion, not much. It is two in the morning. I am having a conversation with a 40-something dude in latex. I say again, "The humiliation is over."

"I know, I get it. But I don't own the key."

"You don't what?"

"I don't own the key to my collar."

"So when is she coming to get you?"

"I don't ask my mistress questions, I said already."

"OK, I dunno, John. I give up."

"It's cool, don't feel bad."

"See you later, I guess."

I look back when I get to the door and it looks like he's already forgotten me.

I go inside the building. They keep it cold, because my guess is that helps keep refrigeration costs down. The floors

21

are all hard, either tile or cement. A couple guys are like, "Did you see out front?" and I shrug because on no level is John actually my problem.

I have to pack my own truck, but the people who work in the warehouse bring all the correct amounts out presorted on wooden palettes, which makes the actual packing part not that brain intensive. We pack almost 150 gallons of six different varieties of milk, buttermilk and milk substitutes such as oat milk and almond milk; four dozen containers of Grade-A eggs; 18 cases of plastic water bottles (because we hate the planet, maybe?); 18 bottles of orange juice; and two cases of half & half genuine dairy creamer.

On the way out, I toss John a bottle of water. I worry because it might make him pee himself. But he's a big boy, he can take care of himself, and maybe he'd be into that sort of thing anyway.

I steer the Moo Cow truck south from the distribution center. In Aspenroot and its suburbs, no one ever says turn right or left. I think this is because the mountains are always visible off to the west, and they give you a way to orient yourself which is guaranteed to be both 100% unchanging and 100% correct.

Our lives are shaped by the geography of our childhoods. I think about this all the time.

What does it do to a kid in San Diego to wake up every morning and know that, some short distance west, there is a line past which you can never walk, and an infinite amount of distance past that line is the horizon behind which the sun will repeatedly disappear?

What does it do to a kid in Nebraska, knowing every year cracked dirt is going to soften and then little lively squiggly shoots will break through, wiggle their way into the air, green reaching up to sky, green spreading out to the horizon?

What does it do to a kid in Kansas to wake up and see perfectly level horizons in every direction, knowing that if he or she spins around a few times, the view will never change, and there will never be a way for him or her to know if he or she is facing west or east or north or south?

That's almost how it was for me, growing up where I grew up, which was basically in the desert. There, our suburbs were strange and quiet places, houses all low and white adobe, the streets very, very wide. There were places I could go to stand and, sure, there might be a spire off to the south or a cactus grove to the left, but at dusk, when the sky got purple and the dirt got black, those geographic markers would disappear and it felt like the walls had been knocked off the world. Like there was no container, no safe space, nothing that stood between me and everything everywhere. The sky above was no more or less infinite than the world below, everything flat and forever lonely.

When I had to move away from the desert in a major post haste, I chose to run to Aspenroot because I needed a fresh start. This was an easy story to tell my parents and my friends, because it felt like a possible truth. And in a way, it was true.

Every day of every year, a flood of young adults chase their dreams to Aspenroot, which is currently the biggest city in America. Most of these young adults are chasing dreams of no-collar life, of working alongside content creators and tech entrepreneurs and experimental architects. Others are drawn by something else, a chapter from a book they read or a scene from one of the dozens of movies filmed in and about Aspenroot every year. Or maybe they have a story in their heads, that they may not make it to the top of this town, but one night, with a cold wind blowing and Christmas bells ringing, they might kiss the love of their life standing on one of its thousands of concrete corners and at that climactic moment the camera will pull away and the music will swell and that one story, theirs, will end happily.

Aspenroot is also currently the biggest city in the world, which makes sense because it was pitched in the middle of the richest country in the world. It is also the highest major city in the nation, a city where the people quite literally live closer to stars.

The Rocky Mountains create a natural wall west of Aspenroot. Multiple walls, in fact, each taller than the last. First the foothills and then the low mountains and then the continental divide past that. Some days I imagine the earliest settlers coming across those flat Kansas plains, wheels turning over easy grasses, and the settlers suddenly seeing all those looming walls and just saying, "Oh, hell no.

This spot right here? This is fine. Let's just build our city here."

And so it was that Aspenroot built itself up fast, some say almost overnight. The settlers built a church and a saloon and then, just like that, a hundred skyscrapers that climbed on top of others, skyscrapers like tumbleweeds piling up against a windbreak.

That same sheer imposing mountain wall that stopped the settlers has defined everything Aspenroot has done since. The way the city talks about distance and direction, the way it plans its streets. The way its residents live their lives. The way wave after wave of young people chase their dreams until this exact point, at which point they stop.

Everything that happens has to happen right here.

The streets that connect Aspenroot's suburban neighborhoods are always so straight, and in the daytime you'd be forgiven for thinking these streets might run and run, run on until they run right into the eastern horizon or the western wall. At night these same straight streets are regularly lit by streetlights placed on central medians, interspersed with aspen and pine. And all cars must drive from circle of light into ocean of darkness and then reappear in the next circle of light as if the street is a filmstrip and the cars are skipping forward from one frame to the next. And if you drive fast enough, only then can you stop seeing the frames and instead imagine an unbroken path ahead.

Drive slow though, you start to see the gaps in the

story.

On the other hand, I can drive the route from Moo Cow back to my hood with my eyes closed. I mean this quite literally. There are no alignment issues with the Moo Cow truck. The street is perfectly straight. No one is ever on it at 2:56 in the morning.

There are a number of stone signs to the left and right and left and right and left and right saying things like "Brandy Estates" or "Burnview" or "Blueberry Heights." Because you have to realize, these very straight streets connect a series of very twisty neighborhoods.

This is important to the story.

When I turn into my neighborhood, Winegrove, that's when everything changes. Every custom home is a bit different, every street weaves and curves, hiding the next house from sight. The houses aren't very far apart; the streets are just very well planned.

I have been the milkman for my own neighborhood for a few months. I have to wear my Moo Cow shirt and I choose to also wear the optional Moo Cow baseball hat low over my face. I don't want my neighbors to recognize me on their doorbell cams.

When I bought my house, the real estate agent told me most of my neighbors had installed We Are Recording brand doorbell cameras. And she apologized my house didn't have one yet, since a quality WAR cam was becoming pretty standard in suburban homes like mine.

But whether they used WAR or some lesser brand, I'm

pretty sure my neighbors wouldn't have recognized me, had they for some unfathomable reason decided to play back footage of their milk delivery. But now, post-party at my house, I wonder. I try to stick to the shadows and keep my head down as I fulfill standing orders and custom requests in the darkness.

Until today, this is the only way I've had to get to know my neighbors.

This family must have a lactose-intolerant kid because all they ever get is almond milk. They live in a house that is white on the sides and back but has a brick facade that I would call communist-bloc gray.

That family must have about 35 children because they go through two gallons of whole milk a week. Also they have a Mercedes van that is maybe too tall for their garage because it is basically permanently parked on the street. This van is not a minivan. It is a full-size people-mover. I want to assume they are Catholic or Mormon, but that might be racist?

And this other family must travel a lot, because they are always drawing a black thick line through their order sheet with a black crayon and writing in black block letters, "No delivery this week, thanks!" Their house has lots of windows, but the shades are always drawn except for a big window way up on the third floor, through which I can see an art deco chandelier. It is nice of them to add "thanks" onto their order sheet. I imagine they are very tolerant people.

Once I get to my little corner of Winegrove, it's amusing to connect faces with houses, but I am very careful to keep my own face shielded because I very much don't want my new friends (?) to catch me, and then ask me why their neighbor (who owns a fancy home just like theirs!) delivers the milk on late Saturday nights / early Sunday mornings.

Somewhere in the middle of my route I get to the home of the Corals. The dad who lives there's name is Jacob. And at my party Jacob, pretty drunk, told me and a whole room full of people an absolutely crazy story.

His wife, whose name I either didn't catch or forgot, was at my party but was not in the kitchen at the time.

Chapter 4
The Story of the Super Slaughter

"The luckiest lovers in the world met at a Christmas party, so full of themselves, so sure the world was wonderful, and very prettied up for the occasion.

"I'd arrived on a direct flight from the Big Apple, not twenty-four hours prior. I was the hotshot, the wunderkind, the boy wonder of SuperMeme/NYC, where management had given me an office with windows and a golden card which entitled me to unlimited lattes at a coffee shop just across Hudson Street. I'd hopped a plane, flown over the flyover states, and arrived in Aspenroot to participate in a full-week brainstorm with SuperMeme's local team. For this party I wore a gray jacket and a rakish red scarf and tight jeans with black boots. I had thick hair I wouldn't dream of combing and cigarettes in my breast pocket, even though I didn't smoke.

"And she? A princess in lavender! Hair that reached the ceiling and heels that stabbed red carpets. A princess with angel eyes and a witch's grin. Her daddy may've gotten her the internship, but she'd turned it into a job all by herself, charming hearts and cutting throats from the moment she walked through the revolving doors of SuperMeme/ Aspenroot. Her skin was smooth, well-kept and pale, though she spent Saturdays sailing Lake Roman and Sundays jogging the Strawberry Peak trail. Beneath her satin dress she wore panties that would have sent her ancestors screaming back aboard the Mayflower.

"Oh, to be twenty-five forever!"

This Jacob guy could 100% tell a story! Everyone's eyes were wide and I was still holding a martini shaker vertically over a glass. The martini had poured out long ago, but I hadn't realized it because Jacob was holding court, just loving the control he had over us, his audience.

This ability to tell a story is something I very much admire.

"We met first with our eyes and then by the bar. I angled my body casually rearward, left elbow cocked on the mahogany countertop, right palm cradling my cocktail. She held her purse with both hands behind her back and turned her torso almost imperceptibly from side to side.

"And the way we conversed, it drew circles around circles. Sentences heavy on double entendres. Eggnog heavy on the rum. Oh, is that mistletoe? Silly me! Now we have to kiss.

"And we kissed with such momentum we fell into an elevator. And the elevator was so fast it tossed us into an office where the door simply flew shut of its own accord.

"We tried to take our time, but neither of us was especially good at it. It wasn't seconds till I was grunting and she was screaming and the desk beneath us was banging, banging loud against the wall. And so we were hidden from a grunting and a screaming and a banging of a different sort altogether."

The crazy thing, there was nothing salacious about this story. Nothing gross about this guy talking about the illicit sex he'd had with some girl. He'd turned himself into a character in a much larger story which was going, we realized suddenly with various levels of memory and recognition, somewhere very, very bad.

"For downstairs," he continued, "the massacre of the century had begun. Slaughterhouse Aspenroot. The Great American Abattoir. Let the devil take the hindmost and a fire eat the rest. One door in, no way out. Forty-six of the forty-eight employees of SuperMeme/Aspenroot and a half-dozen caterers (and the like) punched bloody by a combined five hundred and seventy-three rounds from an AR15 and five semiautomatic pistols.

"The lambs tried to hide under appetizer tables, as if shrimp and olives could bounce back bullets. They cowered behind curtains, and the red of their blood made painterly splashes across white linen.

"Seven of them packed into a corner, made themselves into one big body, pressed up against each other as rounds plowed through one and right on into the next, and in this manner ten bullets erased seven souls. Such efficiency!

"Not a single employee was found on his or her knees, mercifully executed with a single shot to the skull. There'd been no time for begging or prayers on this multi-minute train to hell. It was simply carnage on the grandest of scales.

"And the last body was the killer's own, found alone in the coat closet he'd crawled into. Ass on the floor, slouched against the door, teeth marks on his pistol, brains creating splatter art on the coats surrounding him. There the coroner would bodybag a man named Christopher Gouldberg. He'd been recently dismissed after a dozen years of service in the Aspenroot office's design department. At his apogee some years ago, he'd been made associate creative director, but he couldn't cut the mustard, and so he'd been disrespectfully demoted to senior art director. He'd been tucked away on a crappy client for a half-decade and finally asked to leave because a new executive creative director just didn't need grumpy, failed, old, boring legacy talent interfering with his hot-shit game plan to set the world on fire. Or something of the sort.

"Besides myself and my petite putain, there was a third survivor of the event America's news networks would controversially term the Super Slaughter. Yes," he said, watching some of the locals in his audience nod. "Yes, you've got it. That very Super Slaughter. I was there. And so was a man named Joe Mead. Joe was the guard on duty at Thompson Tower Annex III that night. He heard the first bang and jumped high in his stool. But he didn't move, and who could blame him? Most security guards, after all, would simply assume it'd been nothing more than the sound of a cork dislodged from a bottle of Dom. And the screams were probably just girls who'd been soaked by the foam. The second bang? A firecracker, surely. And the subsequent five hundred seventy-one let loose over eight minutes and forty-four seconds? I have my theories, yes. But whatever the case, it wasn't till after the banging had stopped that Joe Mead abandoned his stool and wandered back to the party calling out, 'Is everybody all right in there?'

"When he swung the door open, he found himself paralyzed. Numb. Useless from the shoulders down and an idiot from the neck up. After a minute or so, Joe took a step into the room and called again, 'Is everybody all right?'

"Which they quite obviously were not.

"Joe Mead took his cell phone from the deep side pocket of his cargo pants and dialed 911. The operator answered and Joe cried at her with terror that wasn't fake or even half-fake, 'I'm at Thompson Tower! Annex III! You have to send help! There's been a shooting! There's been a lot of shooting!' His voice is clear as a bell upon the recording the news outlets were to play over and over for days after. But what you can only barely hear on that famous 911 call was us. For it was at that precise moment that we, the princess in lavender and the duke of New York, came down the elevator with fabulous hair and sloppy crotches. We walked back into the party and just fucking screamed."

My right hand was still holding that martini shaker vertically over my glass. The ice in it had melted and dripped down, ruining the drink beneath. I slowly set it back down and when I let go, I found my fingers had gone numb.

Chapter 5
Identity

When I arrive back at Moo Cow, John is still leashed up. The sunshine is now coming from a higher angle, no longer long horizontal rays but the type of direct light that could give you a burn. I wonder if John has on sunscreen, but I don't ask because I don't feel like talking. I wave to him as I swing the truck through the gates and into the backlot.

He waves back. He seems happy.

I have to tally everything I took with me vs. everything I brought back and this process takes me nearly half an hour. By the time it is over and I leave, John's mistress person has finally come to get him. I wonder if his punishment is over or just beginning, but then on the other hand, it's kind of gross to imagine either way. I ride my bike fifteen miles back to Winegrove and am back in my house by ten a.m..

This is how I spent my Sundays in college, which is

now a few weird years in my rearview mirror:

I woke up and oftentimes my girlfriend, whose name was Mandy, was lying there and she'd wake up too and then we'd have sex. Mandy, like probably a lot of 20-year-old college girls, had just gotten comfortable with her body and she absolutely wanted to screw as much and in as many ways as possible. We'd have sex for as long as I could keep it up, which I was pretty good at for a college guy. We could have sex for an hour or two. Then we'd walk upstairs in boxer shorts and t-shirts.

I lived in this two-floor house and my room was in its basement and oftentimes my five roommates were already up and playing video games in the main room, kinda complaining about how drunk they still were or how hungover. So me and Mandy would go get everybody tacos. We'd come back and everybody would eat tacos and watch football or stare at our phones. Then me and Mandy would go back down to my room and have sex some more and then she'd go back to her sorority house and I'd go to the gym or for a bike ride. When that was done, me and my friends would talk about what party or bar we'd go to next weekend, and then maybe, maybe I'd study for 30 minutes. Maybe.

That was pretty much every Sunday for four years.

It is hard for me to square that human with the human I am now. Maybe the two of us are non-squarable.

This is how I spend my Sundays now:

My milk delivery rounds over, I sit at home and bounce

a tennis ball off the ceiling. If I throw with my left hand and aim for the wall about a foot down from the ceiling, the ball will bounce up into the ceiling and then back down at a steeper angle, into my right hand, so it traces an infinity loop in the air.

Sometimes I fall asleep and I nap straight through till dinnertime. Other times, I take my basketball to the hoops at the school in my hood, and shoot until I feel sleepy. I didn't play basketball in high school, but I'm getting pretty good at it, though I only ever play against myself.

Today, as I bounce the tennis ball off the ceiling, I think about the story Jacob told at my housewarming party. I think about it, tell it different ways to myself till Jacob's breath wasn't stained by my red wine and awesome (for real) mixed drinks. (For real! I spent a bunch of time before the event learning to mix Manhattans and Banhattans and Mindhattans, etc.)

I think about his story till it gets way better than it almost certainly was. I do this frequently, rearrange stories in my head until I like them.

The one thing that keeps tripping me up, though, is the middle of the story. Did the security guard really just sit there all that time? Enough time to let all those people die? It doesn't make sense. No matter how I retell Jacob's story, I can't figure out how a security guard sat around listening to the entirety of a 500-something-round shooting spree.

An awful thought creeps in. Maybe this Jacob cat had been making it up. Maybe he was just entertaining himself by earning and then manipulating an audience. Isn't that what advertising people do professionally?

But there was a coda to the story. Jacob's big reveal, which he made to me alone, in my kitchen, arms around my shoulders, wine breath a bit too hot in my ear, saying despite all the death and stuff, that girl, Kristy Lee McIllvinney, was still the girl he thought about whenever he was alone, in the shower, in a hotel room, after his wife and kids had gone to bed, whatever. Even with all that death, he said, that night - Christmas Eve, the Super Slaughter, whatever you called it - that night was still the best night of his life. It had been, the way he remembered it, the day he looked the best, felt the coolest, won the prettiest girl, had the best sex. It was the day Jacob Coral felt most alive. And a year or two later he even moved out to Aspenroot full-time to try to recapture the magic, even though it meant quitting his job and finding a lesser agency to work for.

He even tried to reconnect with Kristy Lee.

"And? Did you find her?"

And he claimed that he did. That they'd had a drink while a rainstorm had raged outside. But inside, it just fizzled out was all. There wasn't any spark. Maybe the memory of all that death, it was just too much to risk retriggering. Maybe the years had changed them both into different people. Maybe they didn't like each other in the daylight. Who knows? He'd paid her tab, he said. They'd hugged goodbye, he said. He met another woman and they bought a house in the suburbs, a house right near mine.

That sounded authentic. Sad, but authentic.

The way I see it, lying on my floor, bouncing a tennis ball off the ceiling, letting a Sunday day drift by, the way I see it is no day is any more important than any other day. It isn't like a house, where some bricks matter and others you can pull out without much really happening to the overall structure. Every day is important, the day you are born, the day you lose your virginity, the day you spend watching sports on TV and no one talks to you and you don't talk to anyone. All of it matters equally, no matter what my neighbor claimed.

So maybe he hadn't been making it up. Maybe he just had some details wrong. Maybe Christopher Gouldberg had locked Joe Mead in a bathroom? Or maybe not as many people died as Jacob had said?

Jacob had been wearing jeans and a t-shirt that literally had the name of his agency, the one he worked for now, embossed on it, right above where his heart ought to be. It wasn't a golf shirt, OK. In fact, it was a pretty well designed t-shirt and if he'd told me it was for a band or a snowboard company I'd totally have believed him. But still, no one wears t-shirts to a party to impress people, right?

Right?

It's hard to say. Mine was the first suburban party I'd ever attended.

I am lying on the beige carpet that'd come with my house and my feet are up on the fireplace. The fireplace also came with the house. It is natural gas, though, which is not as authentic as logs are but is still substantially more authentic than that electric light show thing some people's houses have, where there is like this wavering paper that simulates a fire while a radiator heats up the grille.

(My fireplace isn't on, though. It is the middle of summer. That'd be silly, running your fireplace, natural gas or not, in the middle of summer.)

I pull my phone out of my pocket, because why am I driving myself nuts wondering about whether or not Jacob Coral was messing with me? Nobody can lie to me. I am a Webworld stalker non pareil. Maybe the best Webworld stalker in America.

The reason why I am such a good Webworld stalker is also the story behind my current need for anonymity. But I only ever tell it to myself, because if I told it to anybody else it'd get me killed, quite possibly.

It ends at a diner somewhere near the Nevada-Arizona border.

Chapter 6
The Story of Clyde and Bonnie

It takes two hours for me to find my words. I hitch my hips onto the trunk, settle my sneakers on the bumper, and speak.

"You stub your toe, what do you say?"

We have just finished breakfast at a quiet diner off the edge of the highway. The sun is so tight on the horizon it's easy to mistake it for the mellow glow of some far-off metropolis.

Indistinct summer heat grows from the gravel to wrap around the female's ankles. She takes her hands off the door of the Cadillac and places them – both of them – into her hair. She pulls at it, enjoying the tangles formed by fifteen hours of anarchy. She scrunches her lips and guesses, "Ouch?"

"Yeah, ouch. Why?"

"I don't know. It hurt?"

I shake my head no. "Yeah, it hurt. But why you say it

is, it's involuntary. Ouch is your body trying to expel energy, push pain away. When you say ouch, it makes you feel better."

The female uses her own hair to tug her face back and forth. "So what?"

"You have to look at it like that when a guy hassles you, grabs your ass. It's not like he thinks it's going to make you drop your panties. It's his body's way of dealing with all that pressure so it doesn't get backed up inside."

She sticks out her tongue at me, she opens her eyes and makes them bug like she's a cartoon. She tries to turn, but is met with an onrush of dawn light. She blinks, squints, says, "You been practicing this conversation ever since we left Vegas?"

"Not the whole ride."

"Well, you wasted your time. I don't buy any of it. You don't go gorilla every time a girl walks into a room. In fact, you've been sitting with me in your shotgun for two states and haven't called me baby, much less smacked my ass."

"Yeah," I say. I tap the trunk beneath me. "And look where bottling up all that aggression's got me."

"So what you're actually trying to say is, I shouldn't have shot the douchebag at the bar?"

"Seems like maybe you took advantage of our temporary position of power."

"Temporary? It's pretty permanent, now that Mr. Grab Ass is missing his right foot."

"Left."

"Whichever."

"I'm saying it because if you keep interrupting things to deal with your personal hang ups, our little Bonnie and Clyde act is gonna end in a way we don't want it to end."

"You suck and you're boring, but ok. No more shooting guys for smacking my ass."

"Promise?"

"Promise. But know what?"

"What?"

"You're Bonnie."

"Whatever you say."

"All right, Bonnie. How much we take from my buddies in the bar?"

I, Bonnie, slide down and pop the trunk. It's covered with dry black felt and inside there's handfuls of twenties and tens blowing loose. I slide our shotguns over to one side and drag the briefcase forward from where it shifted during the ride and it seems really heavy. I remember it banging against my thigh when we were running, maybe? I suddenly feel a bruise forming on my leg and also my hand seems to be sore from how tightly I was holding on to the damn thing, but there was so much adrenaline, everything seems like maybe I am making it up, telling myself a story.

I don't pop open the briefcase. Instead I say, "You want to be the man so bad, Clyde, you count it. Maybe I'll go back in, talk to the waitress. Or the hostess. I don't know. They were both kind of hot."

There'd been a whiff of was about the waitress, while

the hostess walked as if her only want was to live until the day she died. They were equally attractive to me, the male, for I did not have a crush, but lived inside one: the big crush, the crush of all women weighing heavy on me.

"You're not going to grab 'em, are you?"

"No."

"Tell 'em you love their tits?"

"Not that either."

"Swear to god, when we were walking down the Strip last night, some nerd screamed, 'I love your tits' at me."

"You blow his foot off?"

"I should've."

"I'm gonna go find someone non-homicidal to talk with."

"Tell 'em you love their tits. Just see where it gets you."

"I'm not going to say that."

"Come on, Bonnie. See how it sounds."

"No."

"Say it to me."

"You going to shoot me in the foot?"

"Say it, Bonnie."

"If it'll shut you up."

"Fucking say it."

"I love your tits."

And this is the first time we kiss. Clyde pushes her tongue hard into my mouth, feels around in there. When she's done, she reaches into the trunk, past the briefcase, past the tens and twenties, hoists up one of the shotguns, and says, "I got an idea."

"We can't rob the diner."

"Why not?"

"We just ate breakfast there."

"So? We paid cash."

"But they're just people."

"Yeah, and we're outlaws!" she crows.

I try to think of a good comeback and can't and so I grab the second shotgun, which is identical in every way, and run across the parking lot after her.

God, she is so beautiful, the way her sandals kick up gravel and her jean shorts and her black top clings to her shoulders and her slender neck and the freckles. Clyde has long hair and it whips into her mouth as she laughs, but there is nothing she can do to stop it because that shotgun, full-size and worn wood, is heavy and must be held tight in the delicate fingers and the pink-painted nails and the sterling silver rings of her pretty young hands.

The bell rings when we kick through the door and Clyde turns around and opens fire, simply lets loose with laughter and a shell, and the bell and the glass behind it are gone like they never were. She spits hair from her mouth and says, "Hey blondie, give us money."

Blondie is the waitress and she must be forty, dressed in white canvas sneakers and a truck-stopping dress. She doesn't hear Clyde's command, because her ears are ringing shotgun reverb. Her mouth had opened to greet the new customers, us, and now it is frozen that way.

Behind her, a sixty-three-year-old woman has reflexively raised her hands high into the air above her head. As she allows them to creep down, she remembers (perhaps) she has not been able to lift them beyond parallel for several months due to a tennis injury.

To her left, a financial consultant opens his eyes to find he has thrown his body over that of his three-year-old daughter. For the rest of his life (I bet) he will remember this moment when he doubts his essential heroism or parenting skills.

A longtime fry cook crashes hard through the back door of the diner and sprints fifty yards into the sunlight before he stops, his chest throbbing and his hands trembling. He looks left and right, spins all around searching for a phone from which to call the police. He is perplexed when he notices that somewhere between the grill and the door, he must have paused to pick up his cell and his keys and wallet along with it. (I don't know how I know this. I guess I just imagine there has to have been a fry cook back there, somewhere.)

The hostess, an eighteen-year-old girl determined to get out of this town before she becomes the waitress, turns away from the door; she halts only when she realizes she's reaching for the stack of menus, which is what she has always done every time the bell rings. But there are no new customers for her to serve. There is only the waitress and the hostess and the financial consultant and his daughter and the sixty-three-year-old woman and me and Clyde.

"She said, 'Give us your money!'" I shout. I rack my shotgun for effect, accidentally sending a perfectly good shell somersaulting out of the chamber and clacking to the floor. Hearing I have dropped something, I squat down to pick it up, an act for which the waitress thoughtlessly thanks me.

"Oh my god, shut up," Clyde shrieks at her.

"Do what she says," I say, "or she'll blow your foot off."

I try not to laugh, but it's too late. Clyde lowers her shotgun. "What the fuck?"

I apologize, "Sorry, it just slipped out."

The female huffs, she racks, she swings the barrel up and levels it at the waitress. "The money, let's have it." Clyde's little body shifts left and right as she pushes her sandals firmly into the floor and pulls the stock of the shotgun tight into her shoulder.

There is little money in the register, but that is wholly beside the point. We run for the Cadillac, pockets thick with small bills and quarters and even pennies.

I get behind the wheel out of habit and Clyde slides beside me. She slams her door and shoves her face out the passenger window and laughs an insane laugh, a laugh instantly stolen by the engine and the tires. And then she pulls herself into a ball and slides on sunglasses and the two lenses of the sunglasses connected by the tiny curve of the nosebridge create an infinity symbol across Clyde's face. I can see this infinity symbol in the rearview mirror and also see myself reflected in it twice, once on her left lens and once on her right lens, my two faces looking back at me in the mirror.

At some point, she probably falls asleep. I, though male, can not blame her. Sleep, too, is an involuntary thing.

We had met at a resort wedding in Scottsdale fifteen hours earlier. I had arrived alone, a past boyfriend of the bride. She was a cousin of the groom, and had come with her father and mother and sister, too. She'd wandered to the pool where she found me lounging on a chair, my first Mai Tai already half gone. I immediately confessed I was not altogether comfortable with the idea of watching another male carry away my ex, and she found me grumpy and adorable, all uncombed hair and desert ease. After an hour we'd dared ourselves to collect her father's Cadillac from the valet and drive like hell, five hours northwest to Las Vegas. We'd bender all night and return in the morning before anyone noticed our absence. Neither of us had wedding duties or any reason to remain sober.

This was a thing that could be done.

The shotguns were her father's. He'd packed them on the off-chance there was an opportunity to shoot clays at the resort. She discovered them in our trunk by accident, much to the future dismay of the douchebag at the bar.

And now my male heart starts to pound as I drive south along Mojave, trying to find an eastbound highway that will take us towards Scottsdale. I count the reasons this might be.

1. I have been awake for twenty-four hours.

2. I have downed a half-dozen cocktails.

3. I lost $600 playing roulette.

4. I stole some briefcase from a bar on the south edge of the Strip, just after I watched a girl (who I do not know) shoot a douchebag's foot off.

5. I robbed a diner staffed by not one but two beautiful women.

6. I kissed a pretty girl, or rather let her kiss me, and I feel something strange and wonderful has begun.

At any time, flashing lights might appear behind us. At any time, the sun might scratch Clyde awake and she might unball herself and open her arms and stretch her ribs. The highway is a straight shot into the empty hours in front of us. I keep one hand steady on the wheel and look at the female for what seems like minutes at a time. I consider stealing her, kissing her awake after we have crossed some border into a foreign land where any amount of American dollars would let us live out our lives like kings.

And queens.

I (or Bonnie or Rob or whatever the female will call me when she wakes) check my rearview mirror and in it I see only my own reflection and the words, "Objects are closer than they appear."

If we do reach the resort, if we slide through the foyer and into my room unnoticed, friends and family may whisper, but nothing more. Perhaps on their ten-year anniversary, the bride and groom will laugh over how Danica and Rob hooked up at their wedding. It will all become a rumor, a story, gossip shared purely because people can't help themselves.

Chapter 7
Erasure

And then the next day, me and Danica walked out into blinding desert sunshine, completely hungover, fucked out, scented with sand and sweat and her pussy and my semen and so much sunscreen and so much saliva and so, so, so much alcohol. We walked out sticky, only to find the money from the suitcase, the tens and twenties, was on top of a false bottom and underneath the false bottom was hundreds. And the hundreds numbered in the hundreds. And moreover, twelve kilo bars of gold. And moreover than that, a bag full of diamonds.

Danica and me split the gold in half. And then she gave me two extra bars as a way of apologizing for her shooting someone. She let me have all the diamonds and the velvet baggie they came in, too. And then she impulsively reached two long fingers into the baggie and pinched one out. She held it up to my nose and said, "Now we're married." She waited for a second and said, "Psyche," and laughed at me. She put that diamond in her pocket and let me keep the rest. This was easy for her to do though, since her daddy was and probably still is some sort of billionaire.

We kissed goodbye, not a passionate kiss, more like a promise. Her lips tasted like salt and her breath was sour with all the alcohol.

This whole story is likely to be at least partially untrue, given that I alter it every time I tell it just slightly so as to delight the audience, which is only ever me. But the substance of the matter is, I did suddenly and via violence come into possession of a bag of diamonds and eight kilo bars of gold, which is both more and less than it sounds.

Kilo is the average weight people buy when they are buying gold to store it in a safety deposit box or something. It's not, like, a brick. It's more like the size of a chocolate bar. So they aren't all that impressive. But these bars were valued, eventually, at a bit more than 50k apiece. And it's less hard to sell gold bars than it is to sell, say, heroin. (That's just an assumption on my part of course.)

It's a snap to sell diamonds.

It is less of a snap to shake the conviction that a vengeful gem thief might murder you. Or that cops might arrest you for knocking over a diner.

I didn't think anyone from the bar or the diner would recognize me. But I started going by Bob anyway. And I didn't shut down my social channels, which probably would have made more of a ruckus than what I did do, which was I went on whatever accounts I had and posted saying I needed to take a break from social media for a while. Then I just never went back. I figure anyone who did go to my accounts just figured my life was better without them, which is why I never posted and is something pretty much everybody kind of suspects to be true anyway. That makes it easy to believe, and that's the key to a great lie, remember. It's very close to the truth.

And more importantly, I moved away from Arizona, where I'd been knocking around, interning and clerking, figuring out what to do with my college degree and country club connections, and I bought a house in a suburb of Aspenroot, which seemed like a distinctly non-armed-robber-like thing to do. I didn't have enough cash to live on forever, but I could slack off for a few years, figure things out.

I often checked up on/stalked Danica on social media, just to make sure she hadn't mysteriously disappeared, fallen into a pit of alligators, or been found stabbed in an alleyway with the words "YOU'RE NEXT, ROB/BOB" chalked above her corpse. But mostly she just posted selfies of herself wearing a bikini on the prows of various sailboats, but she'd been doing that since before we met, so I didn't worry a ton about it. Oftentimes in these photos she would be raising a drink of some sort, sort of saluting the camera, perpetually toasting Webworld with the Amalfi coast or someplace like that behind her.

I also went to anonymous computers that couldn't be traced back to me, computers at libraries and stuff, and did a whole lot of Webworlding to figure out just who we'd robbed. I cross-referenced bars and hospital reports. I read police reports about dead bodies that popped up. But I never found one about a guy who'd been an enforcer for a certain mob type who'd had his foot shot off and then been shot in his head in what no one would ever know were two separate shootings. (Except, of course, me and Danica and whoever shot him in the head as punishment for, I assume, losing all that gold and all those diamonds to two drunk idiots on a bender on their way back to a wedding in Scottsdale.) Point is, after a lot of digging, I still wasn't sure who we'd robbed or if we really got away with it.

So whenever I left my house in the dark hours of the morning for my job at Moo Cow, I always took my time and stayed aware of my surroundings, just in case some dude without a foot should come limping my way. Or worse, a perfectly ambulatory guy who theoretically offed the dude without the foot.

Anyway, my frequent and totally understandable and non-creepy stalking of Danica and various criminals and court cases made me extraordinarily competent at cyberstalking in general. And five minutes of phone time tells me The Super Slaughter was an extremely real happening.

I guess I'd heard about it before, in retrospect. But in

America's mass of mass shootings, it'd been kind of buried, no pun intended.

Four dozen ad execs got killed, America figures ok, good riddance, maybe?

My neighbor's full name, Jacob Coral, is a really cool name, but I have a hard time squaring the man I'd met with the protagonist of his story. That younger man seemed like a rocketship rider, a blue flamer on his way to the very tip-top of a competitive profession. But maybe tip-top of advertising is a house in this really-nice neighborhood and a well-designed t-shirt? Maybe in advertising that is as good as it gets, which compared to sweating it out in a rice paddy in midland China or something is probably A-OK.

The girl, Kristy Lee McIllvinney, is working in Aspenroot but not in advertising any longer. She has a site up that is about skirts and shoes and her ProPro says she is an art buyer and content creator at the in-house catalog, magazine, blog and branded content publishing arm of Cash Register, which is a global fashion retailer with a hub here in Aspenroot.

The third survivor of the Super Slaughter, Joe Mead, takes much longer to find because his name is so common. I have to go through a bunch of social media sites checking photos against the photo I found in the paper, which showed a kid-like man with a babyfat face and a crewcut that just screamed, "I wish I was in the army." I crawl back through a million now-defunct social networks until I find a profile that looks like him, kind of. The final post, the one at the top, maybe three months after the Super Slaughter, says, "I am taking a break from social media for awhile."

He'd posted that and never come back.

Chapter 8
Isolation

After a half-block I realize I am not dribbling my way towards the basketball courts in my hood, which are also tennis courts, green clay outlined by red clay. Instead, I am heading deeper into Winegrove quite randomly through row after row of houses. I dribble harder than maybe I should or need to, soft hands, hard wrist flick, the concrete giving an echo - pang pang pang. It sounds like I am pounding carpenters nails into the sidewalk. I cross over and go between the legs casually. I feel like I am getting good enough to claim I was "varsity in high school" and maybe even "played a bit of college ball," though that would be risky, given the existence of Webworld. And as I am thinking this, I realize I have come almost full circle and arrived back along my sidewalk, right in front of the short steps leading up to the wide front porch of Jacob Coral, who on this Sunday afternoon is standing on it, the porch, and holding two bottles, one of milk that I may have recently delivered and one of something that looks dangerously toxic, and he holds this second bottle up and away from his body so he won't spill it as he leans down and pours the first bottle, the one of milk, into a plastic bowl.

"Jacob," I say.

And he says in a deeply blissed-out way, "Bob, man. You finished cleaning up our mess yet?"

The mess wasn't that bad. Actually, it wasn't much of a mess. It was more like a few dozen bottles I dumped into my recycling bin. But I don't tell him this. Instead I say, "You got, like, a cat?"

"Trying to," he says, and waves me up, makes this half pull with his right hand and it takes me a couple seconds to see he is waving me, he is waving me up the walk, but in a way like he has a secret to share.

One time, when I was job hunting, back in Phoenix, I was going to see this intern-needing startup in a section of town I'd charitably call transitional and a woman in torn leggings and a handkerchief hat gave me a similar wave. I had been taught, stop for women, but I also knew I shouldn't get out of my car in this ungentrified section of the city so I braked and locked my doors and rolled down the window only enough I could crane my lips up over the rim and shout, "What?"

So she came trundling down to the street, her head almost lolling side to side with laughter, lolling in time to her buttocks galavanting down towards me to come to stop at the car and she said in a somewhat hushed tone, "You're not supposed to make me come all this way out here, sugar." I went what again and she said, "You looking to score?" I stuttered something, I don't know what I stuttered, like I was looking for an address and was lost, obviously, and she realized her mistake. But I guess when skinny white college boys came to her block, that was what they wanted, most often. To buy drugs. So her confusion was totally understandable.

Anyway, this is the same wave I get from my new buddy.

This is progress. I hold my basketball palm up, balancing it as I walk up the steps and sit in the chair where Jacob points me. He half-falls into his Winegrove regulation porch swing and says, "Melinda, she was so hung over this morning. She was trying to make the kids breakfast, we all ended up going to IHOP and she just sat there. It was brutal."

I guess getting your neighbor's wife hammered is OK, but I don't say anything witty because I need to make another mental note to make a real note to remember that Jacob's wife is Melinda and not to confuse her with Mindy, who is my next-door-neighbor whose name I don't know's wife.

Jacob sees me staring at the bowl of milk and says, "Mice," as if that solves it.

"You have mice?"

"Under the porch, man. Melinda wants me to kill them, but poison, think about that. It could get into the groundwater, I don't know. And then those little glue traps they sell? Barbaric shit. So I figure if I can get the neighbor's cat to hang out, maybe it'll eat the mice for me, I won't have to do anything."

"What if the cat starts to, like, 'hang out' hang out?"

Jacob reaches down beside him where there is a cooler and he opens it and passes me a beer.

I look at the beer, I look at the milk.

Jacob says, "Josie's goat monster will get it."

And he laughs at this and I wonder, is the joke on me or am I the joke?

He sees me not laughing. "No for… Wait… Josie didn't tell you about the goat monster?"

I just look at him.

"Man, she tells everybody about the goat monster. She was at your party and she didn't say anything, she is making real progress."

She was at my party? I don't think I ask this out loud.

Jacob looks a bit off the porch. The railing is white picket, the way cottages in, like, the seashore communities of North Carolina are white picket, probably, the slats of the fence opening up to show you so much white sand beyond them.

"The other day, the Suppervilles, you know them right?"

I make a noncommittal shrug, like who doesn't know the Suppervilles, right?

"Yeah, right, there was that whole wife-swapping party

rumor? Them. But so they lost their cat the other day. Got hit by a car or got sick of listening to Greg make awkward comments about his wife's boobs. And she posted on the Winegrove Hoodlife page, has anybody seen her cat? And Josie gets on and goes off. She says she saw this goat monster come running up on her porch and eat the cat. Like, this massive furry thing."

"Like a coyote."

"No, she talks about it all the time. Like gray and furry."

"Sounds like a coyote."

"It's not a coyote."

"OK."

"On its hind legs, with horns on its head."

"Oh."

"Right, so everyone is sort of making fun of her so Josie says no, she can prove it, because it's on her WAR cam because it was triggered by the motion sensor or whatever. And she posts the film to Hoodlife but come on, it's a motion camera doorbell cam and it's night. It's like, a blur, could be a UPS guy and a leaf on the ground. People start trying to mess with her and say, like, it's a ghost or no it's a werewolf. And Josie was so pissed. Oh my god. Swears it's a goat on two legs eating the Supperville's cat on her porch and anyone who sees anything else is deluding themselves."

"Huh."

"I saw it, I saw a milkman chasing a rolling bottle of milk. But what do I know?"

"A milkman?"

"Dude, it could've been a kid ding-dong ditching her. Dude, you know how bad those WAR cams are."

"Actually..."

"A hold out, huh? Good for you. I guess. Fuck them, recording us and..." Jacob does not so much trail off as suddenly and abruptly screech to a word halt.

I realize I am supposed to drink this beer he has handed me and all of a sudden I need to. I take a drink and can't really say if it is good or not, but I smile nonetheless.

"What are you drinking?" I ask.

It turns out his toxic-looking beverage is actually kombucha tea that Jacob is drinking because he is extremely high on pot brownies. He asks if I want one and I say yeah. He disappears into the house and comes back and says, "Melinda makes them but she has to hide them in a broccoli package, so the kids don't eat them by accident. I guess they wouldn't really be able to get to them, they're little still. But still, can't be too careful."

"Good thinking," I say. This is awkward and to make up for it I take a bite of brownie. It tastes just like a brownie.

"Dude, this is a pot brownie? It's good."

He laughs at me, "Better watch out, the WAR cams don't have speakers yet, but your phone's listening."

"Who's listening?"

"I am, man. Advertisers. You say you like pot brownies, your phone doesn't notify the cops. It notifies me. And I start serving you ads for fucking brownie mix."

"You personally?"

He just sighs. Minutes drift by. Finally, "This neighborhood, man," he says. Then he says, "Neighbooorhood," throwing, I think, some extra o's in there to make a joke about bores or boorishness, but I can't be sure.

I take another bite.

"We live in a bubble, Bob."

"We're pretty lucky," I venture.

"No." He leans forward and puts his forearms on his thighs and looks right at me. "Literally. There's a ceiling over this neighborhood. Like, a fake sky they put up there to trick us."

"Like a camping tent?"

"Yeah, look." He is pointing at something very, very precisely. I slowly lean out from the porch and follow his pointer finger up, up into the air.

"See it?"

"Kind of blue?"

"No, look. You can even see the seam along the top of the tent. See right, right there?"

And there is a line, once I know where to look. I think it's connecting one of the neighbor's roofs to their tree and I'm pretty sure it's a Christmas decoration they forgot to take down. And I think how sad it must be to look at a sky and see only ceiling. But that's precisely when the pot in the brownies starts to kick in. It's a racing sort of buzz, the type that isn't and isn't and then just really, really is. The type that's in all your skins and tissues at once. And about the ceiling, I'm not sure anymore. The thin line suddenly seems very thin and much farther away. And come to think of it, why isn't the wind blowing on this wonderful sunny afternoon? Where is the atmosphere, if we're really outside? Where is the noise? Shouldn't it be, I don't know, louder? Shouldn't there be some sort of noise?

I fall back in my seat, drink some of the beer Jacob gave me. I feel very warm inside.

He says, "Yo, go to movie night with the Suppervilles, and ask Josie about it. I bet she talks your ear off about the goat monster. I bet she does."

"Movie night is at their house?"

"What? No. That Greg, Supperville, who's an insurance agent, he sets it up for the kids summer evenings. At the park." I feel especially dumb as he goes on to say, "Dude, they were at your party. Greg and Dana."

I feel like I should be writing all this down. Jacob and Melinda. Someone and Mindy. Greg Supperville and his wife Dana who has boobs, but they no longer have a cat. The Suppervilles sell insurance and host movie night in the neighborhood park. Josie has a doorbell camera and was potentially the last person to see Greg and Dana Supperville's cat. Is that everything?

Maybe whoever pitched the sky tent heard us talking and unzipped the fly, because suddenly a wind kicks up, and while our Sunday afternoon is hot, there is no such thing as a hot wind in Aspenroot. Wind comes down from the east side of the continental divide, cools over year-round glaciers before making its way east into suburbs such as Winegrove. This wind ripples the milk in the bowl, milk I had probably delivered maybe twelve hours before, for a cat that might never show up to drink it, and, if it does, might get eaten by a goat monster that almost certainly doesn't exist, and this same wind lifts up Jacob's hair and I see, in that moment, a glimmer of the rake he'd been the night of the Super Slaughter.

"Hey," I say, "about that story you told."

He shakes his head and says, "I don't know why. I don't actually like to talk about it, when I'm sober. But it's one of those moments. Keeps turning over in my head. I keep telling it to myself and telling it to myself and sometimes I find myself telling it to other people. Does that, does it make sense," some corporate negotiating storytelling training making him open his hands as he finishes with my name, which is, "Bob?"

I nod. "Totally."

He nods.

"But like, the security guard?"

I see his eyes get bored and flicker out to the sidewalk to see who might be coming, but nobody is. Between all the sex and dying, the security guard is clearly the least important part of this moment in his history. To him, that is. "That Joe Mead guy? Yeah?"

"Like, really, you said he stayed put for eight minutes?"

Jacob shrugs. "I think they say he thought they were fireworks, but you know what I think? I think he knew. I think he knew and was chicken. So he just waited for it all to be over."

"But, like, why wouldn't he call the police? I can see him being too scared to go inside the room, but?"

"But it didn't matter. The bad guy had killed himself. The accountants descended the next day and rectified the books. It was all over."

"The very next day? Christmas Day?"

But Jacob has flattened out, hair flattened out on his skull, body flattened out on his swinging porch swing. He is looking up at the seam in the sky again, puzzling over the vastness of whatever lay beyond the ceiling some unknown string-puller has draped over his adulting.

I look at my watch and count eight minutes, let them go by without a word, just two suburban guys, passing a summer afternoon on a porch, drinking beers, sneaking pot brownies, protected from the cold of the mountain winds by the very same things that hemmed us in.

Eight minutes is an eternity. Sixty-four super measured breaths. Enough time for a kid on a strider bike to go sliding soundlessly past and then for said kid's mother to go clomping after him, her flip-flop steps the only noise we can hear for miles and miles. And at the end of that warm eternity I am surer than ever that the answer to some question I don't know yet is Joe Mead.

Shortly after that, Melinda comes out and joins us for a

minute. Their kids come out of the house, too, but are far too young to be given free rein of the hood and so they do a hot lap or two on the Coral's lawn and then head back inside. Numerous other things happen, people walk dogs on the sidewalk out in front, no mice show up, neither do any cats.

When I leave later on that evening, Jacob is like, "See you at movie night."

I am so shocked I don't know what to say. I had a lot of friends in high school and college. I am not quite sure why I am surprised I have one now.

When I get home the sky and my home are both dark.

My house is a bit smaller than most of the houses in the neighborhood. They did it this way on purpose, made some smaller and some bigger in some ridiculous approximation of diversity, catering to mid-millionaires and high-hundred thousandaires alike. And all my rooms are dark, too, because there is no one there to turn the lights on.

I head up one flight of stairs to my bedroom where I have a fireproof safe I have bolted through the carpet into the wooden floor. In this safe are only two things. A now one-third-full bag of diamonds and a stack of eight gold bars.

I take the bars out, heavy as they are, and I take them into my bathroom and turn that light on over my head. And now I set them, the bars, on the floor one at a time on their short ends so they stand vertical in a line like dominoes. I worry about what happens if I knock one over and eventually, as always, the worrying gets to be worse than the reality and so with a finger I tip the first one into the next, and it falls into the next and so on, one through eight.

To my ears, they sound deafening as they hit the tile. They sound a little bit like gunfire.

I sit on my bathroom floor amongst the fallen gold bars and I look at Danica's social feeds on my phone for an amount of time that probably qualifies as pathetic, wondering what I lost when she drove right out of my life and it started to hurt, a little hurt, one I wasn't sure wasn't just a bit of hunger because all I'd had to eat was the pot brownies Jacob fed me.

I surf Danica's feeds long enough Webworld starts to serve me ads advertising beach vacations, and it doesn't sound so bad, sitting on a beach for some indeterminate amount of time. But then I see my thumb, disconnected from my brain, move across my screen, searching Webworld for photos of Kristy Lee McIllvinney.

Chapter 9
Investigation

After a while, I realized the cool thing about being invisible is I never had to feel self-conscious about being alone. Lots of people won't go to dinner alone, but I will. Or movies. I go to the movies alone if there is something I want to see. The seat next to me always seems to be empty. It's weird. Or bars sometimes. I mean, it is weird to go to a bar alone, but for some reason no one seems to care I'm there. Maybe they all think I'm alone because I'm getting stood up by my friends and/or girlfriend. Probably girlfriend. No one looks at me, maybe because they feel bad for me, but maybe because I am invisible.

Another benefit of being invisible is that I rarely get asked to leave anywhere. I can order a cup of coffee in, say, a coffee bar in the lobby of a large skyscraper, where dozens or even hundreds of businesses plot strategy and marketing etc, and I can sit there for almost all day and not really worry that the security guard is going to wander over and lay a hand on my shoulder while he asks, "Sir, are you visiting someone in the building?"

I take the 888x down to Aspenroot on Monday, very early. The financial crowd, the bankers and the lawyers, are all crowding into downtown, but the no-collar types, the UX designers and the urban planners, they're still kissing their spouses goodbye in whatever suburb they call home, I bet.

The skyscrapers in Aspenroot were all built at once, right next to each other, as if space and air were a resource even scarcer than steel girders and brown-brick facades. And in the rare instances where the buildings aren't leaning drunkenly upon each others' shoulders for support, the alleyways are so skinny you could barely slip a body and a trashcan between them. I walk the sidewalk past these brotherly buildings until I reach Aspenroot's very middle, the gold-sheeted sides of the Cash Register.

Cash Register (the building) is a mammoth structure, home to Cash Register (the business) and also a couple hundred other businesses, most of which can loosely be defined as creative.

I loiter on the sidewalk outside until I am 100% sure the security guard is a big black guy, which is to say he is not Joe Mead. But my cover, such as it is, is almost blown anyway, because when I walk in I am shocked to see the receptionist at the information desk is, I am pretty sure, the same teenager girl who works at Moo Cow.

I dive behind a stone pillar and peek out at her from behind it, which I am sure looks suspicious to the people starting to filter into the building, but I really don't want her to see me, for reasons I can't possibly articulate. What would it matter if she saw me? I don't know.

She has her hair back in a ponytail, which on her really does kind of look like a pony's tail because her hair is thick but very straight, and she hasn't put on makeup or anything, but she doesn't look haggard like she is working two jobs, one at night and another during the day. She just looks like she is sitting at the information desk so if someone were to want to know where Cash Register (the building) leasee Squared Off Stores Inc.'s corporate office was, they could walk right up and ask her and she'd be, like, "Twentieth floor. Up the escalator to the mezzanine, second bank of elevators on your right," super bored and chewing gum the entire time.

As casually as I can, I leave the safety of the pillar and I try to blend in with other business-casual people walking from the street across the atrium past the coffee stand to the escalator to the banks of elevators, except I don't go to the escalator. I peel off at the coffee stand and sit down at one of the four or five little tables they have set up there. I hold my phone up to block my face and look around, wondering what time Kristy Lee McIllvinney might make an appearance.

I don't pull her photo up on my phone. I have already

memorized what she looks like. Like the sun if it were a person. Like a cheerleader in a coming of age film. Like a princess in lavender - isn't that what Jacob said? - grinning a witch's grin.

When she finally enters the atrium, it's like someone turned the thermostat up a couple degrees it's suddenly so much more pleasant. I stand up and slide in behind her and stand in line for coffee with her, but she never notices me, not even after she orders and turns around and bumps right into me. That's how close I am standing. She bumps right into me and says sorry at the same time I say sorry, but her eyes watch the rim of her cup, trying to keep it level. They never meet mine, no matter how much I want them to.

And I want them to very much.

Kristy Lee is just as pretty as Jacob said. There is a ring on her right ring finger, but not her left. There is also a gym bag over her shoulder with a pair of runners knotted to the strap.

I follow her up the escalator to the mezzanine and then she peels off to the right, to stand waiting for an elevator, and I think maybe it's just a step too far to try to ride up with her all the way to whatever floor she gets off on, even if the elevator is packed with people in business casual clothes, holding their bags and their coffees, trying not to look at each other, trying to just get to whatever no-collar jobs they have.

I mean, I may be invisible but I'm a human, so I take up physical space, at least I think.

So instead I veer left and follow the mezzanine rail for about 30 yards until I find the entrance to a hallway. This lonely hallway is very dark, without much in the way of overhead lighting. But I need a place to hide out because I see Kristy Lee is standing, waiting for her elevator and she is starting to look at the faces of the people around her.

And so I step inside.

It's hard to see much for sure in here. My eyes need time to adjust, time to see another world than I saw in that atrium, which was full of sunlight and Kristy Lee. And the hum of the atrium and the buzz of the elevators, those are gone too. The only sound I can identify is the inhalation of an air circulation system that seems to be sucking air from the atrium, pulling it up to the mezzanine and past me down the hall, into the darkness.

I glance behind me and I see there are office doors on either side of this hallway, and they seem to get smaller and smaller as the hallway goes on and on into some unseen infinity, way in the heart of the Cash Register.

I put one hand on the wall to try to orient myself, and find it covered with some sort of velvet wallpaper, soft and either black or so dark that it appears black here in the shadows of this quiet hallway.

Slowly I peek out around the corner, back into the atrium, to see if Kristy Lee has boarded her elevator yet. But apparently I waited too long. My eyes have adjusted to the darkness, and I can't see anything out there at all anymore. It's all just white light and humming. I have to squint as I pull myself out of the hallway and am released into the mezzanine, the escalator, the atrium and finally Aspenroot.

Chapter 10
The Story of the Goat Monster

"Can I tell you a secret, Bob? The most powerful words in the English language are, 'Can I tell you a secret.' No one ever says no.

"That's one secret. Here's another one:

"I hate my WAR cam.

"I hated it before we bought it. I resisted getting it forever. Josh would say, 'Don't you want to know who's at the front door before you get up from the couch?'

"'No.'

"'Don't we want to have a recording if porch pirates take off with our deliveries?'

"'No.'

"'What about if the doorbell rings when I'm away on business? Wouldn't you like to be able to see who it is before you open the door?'

"'Ugh, they're called windows, Josh, and there's literally a window in our door.' And even if we had no windows, even if windows had never been invented, I still didn't want a WAR cam.

"But soon, it was like we were being left out at the cool kids' table. We'd go to parties and WAR was all people would talk about. 'Oh, did you see that teenage driver speed over the speed bump?' 'Oh, did you see the adorable missionaries selling bibles?' 'Oh, did you watch the horny couple kissing in their car? No? Go watch it. Go watch it all! It's waiting on your WAR cam!'

"It was like society had given up on me, like everyone else was addicted to a new show on TV and I didn't subscribe to the right channel. So eventually, I gave up. I told Josh we could get one and I sat there on my couch, arms crossed and legs crossed, pouting as two men in blue trousers installed it and Josh signed something and away they went, leaving us this brochure on how to download the WAR app so we could stream through our phones. 'WAR flips on when the motion sensors get triggered!' 'WAR comes with optional sync to your door chime!' 'Rewind and watch WAR at your convenience!'

"You want to know a secret, Bob? Once you start watching WAR, you can't stop.

"It is the greatest show on earth and the best part is that it happens on my personal stage. Every day, a line of characters comes knocking at my door! Converts and salesmen and package delivery technicians. And they stand there so obediently, hands folded while they wait for me to answer the door. Which I don't because I'm never home during the day anyway. I'm at work. And every time my phone vibrates I take it out of my pocket and presto, my favorite show is on again! Starring some scrawny kid with a stack of cookie boxes. Or a missionary in his black pants and white shirt. The delivery drivers dropping off their packages, kneeling to place them upon my doormat.

"Every once in a while, one of them will sit down on our porch furniture, stare down at the concrete between their feet, just rest there for a few minutes, not even knowing - *I am watching.*

"Pretty soon, I stopped putting my phone away at all. All I did was sit there in my office with my phone out, holding it in both hands, holding the WAR Live Now! Button down with my thumb so I could see whatever my house saw.

"And then, one night, the goat monster came.

"I was asleep but I must have been sleeping so lightly, just drifting on sleep's edges, because I heard my phone rattle on the nightstand. My hand shot out and picked it up and squeezed. I wasn't ashamed! I just didn't want it to wake up Josh, that was all! I lay there in the blackness just breathing, saying, 'Don't look at it, Josie. It's probably just the milkman. It's probably just the milkman. Don't look. Don't look.' And I had almost beaten it, beaten back the hunger - the craving - to open up my WAR app when I realize, it can't be the milkman, because our milkman comes on Saturday.

"It is the middle of the night. And there is a stranger

on our porch.

"I wrap myself up in my robe and in bare feet I get up and sneak down the stairs, holding onto the bannister with one hand, the other holding my phone up to my face, my eyes letting in less and less light as they adjust to the bright light of the screen. And I open the app and hold the WAR Live Now! Button.

"But there's nothing there.

"I'd never tried to stream my WAR cam at night before. Oh Bob, it's a different world. The lens isn't so good without light. Everything is pixels, everything is gray. Shades of gray on pink on black. And in the daylight, I can see all the way across the greenbelt, onto the neighbor's porch. But at night, I can only see my own porch, just to the edge of the railing - that's all.

"I got to the bottom of the stairs and snapped on the light without thinking. My front door has a little glass square in it, a window, just a foot or so wide, right at eye height, and all I could see in it was my own reflection. But just like that I realized, I knew, that anything on the other side of my door had a perfect view - *of me*.

"And the darker it was on the other side of that door, the more perfectly framed I became.

"It was silly. It was unlikely and paranoid. And I knew it. I had looked through my WAR! I knew that whatever had been on that porch was long gone. And yet there was this panic attack, this pain. Like a python, every time I went to suck in a breath it took its opportunity to squeeze me a little tighter. My ribs were being crushed because I knew that just a couple minutes ago, *something had been on the other side*. I reached forward and touched the door. It was deadbolted, locked, there was nothing to be afraid of. And yet I could feel something standing out there, out on the street maybe, out where I couldn't see, something looking back at my face hovering in that glass square, seeing me, the way I'd tried to see it.

"I was a character in someone else's show. And now *they* were watching me.

"I ran. I ran back to where I'd turned on the overhead light and I switched it back off and then I stood in the safe dark and scrubbed back through my WAR recordings to find out what had made my phone rattle in the middle of the night," Josie tells me, her sitting on the grass with ankles crossed out in front of her, leaning over and whispering almost into my ear, like her words in this Saturday-night darkness might travel too far and overwhelm the movie and all the happy kids watching it.

"Bob, I saw *this*."

Josie leans over and holds her phone a foot in front of my face. I can smell summertime chardonnay on her breath, she is so close. And she hits the play button, shows me the clip. And I, her slave, watch.

Where there is front porch and front-porch fence, the screen is white and everywhere else there is a fuzzy gray, rose-gray, not pixelated exactly but blurry, like a fog had settled in there around my new friend Josie's home. And then I see a tumbleweed bounce up the steps and blow slow, tumbling to the middle of the front porch. The tumbleweed contracts, an amorphous blob freezing and coiling and swelling at the edges.

And then in stop motion, bigfoot appears, first peering over the railing on the right side of the screen.

Bigfoot hurdles onto the porch and now he is standing there, wavering like a pine tree in stiff winds. The tumbleweed swells and shrinks and then, suddenly, bigfoot reaches down, scoops up the tumbleweed in one long arm, and runs the other way, floating through the fence on the other side of the deck like a ghost and now there's nothing left but a gray-rose fog and the gray-white of the concrete porch.

"See?" Josie says.

And I nod. I saw bigfoot kidnapping a tumbleweed, not a goat monster eating a cat. But the point is, I did see. And so I nod that yes, to my eye, something had been there.

(Also, and mostly, I am glad I didn't see a milkman chasing a rolling bottle of milk, because how awkward would that have been?)

Josie shrugs. Josie shakes her head, so sad. "And then I saw Dana's post and so I shared my WAR footage, to show it was her cat that got eaten on my porch. And nobody believes me, but it's right there. People say it's fuzzy. But it's not fuzzy because it's a WAR cam. It's fuzzy because it's fur, Bob. It's fur."

Chapter 11
Distortion

The movie night movie screen is bright, distorted in the way that projector screens are, the canvas rippling just slightly, the movie stretching slightly across the canvas, so slightly I can't tell: is the stretching horizontal or vertical, are the faces too smushed or the torsos too long, or maybe both at alternate times, dependent solely on the very subtlest of breezes?

I leave Josie and worm my way back through the families sitting in clusters on blankets on the grass, two or three or four or five kids on their bellies on each blanket. One or two pairs of parents on lawn chairs behind them. Cheetos for the kids, plastic cups full of wine for the adults, these same adults slouching lower and lower in their seats as the movie goes on in the night, and slouched lowest among them, towards the back, Jacob and (I remember) Melinda.

He whispers hey and she says hi in a voice not a whisper, a real voice, soft and sweet but bubbly enough to carry, and I crouch down in the grass beside them.

"Josie show you her Zapruder?"

I nod and then, emboldened by the night, I say, "I have to admit, I saw something."

Jacob nods sagely. "People see what they're told to see."

On the screen in front of us, everyone is seeing the same thing: a rhinoceros chasing a popular, muscular action star down a jungle path. For some reason this is funny to everyone. But are we seeing the same thing? If for some reason my whole life I consistently perceived rhinos as elephants and elephants as rhinos, how would I ever know?

"I didn't necessarily see a goat monster," I protest. "More like bigfoot."

Melinda leans across Jacob. I can see in her cup there is some sort of dark liquid. I assume it is red wine. "I saw," she says, "a person. I seriously think it's just a blurry film of UPS or Amazon or whatever and Josie needs to settle the fuck down."

"She told a good story," I say.

"Oh for sure," Melinda says. She leans even farther and now her forearms are basically resting in Jacob's lap. Even in the dark, this close her face is very clear to me and I realize it is really pretty and looks, in fact, a lot like Kristy Lee McIllvinney's face.

Melinda's face just sort of hovers there, her chin inches above her husband's thighs, her eyes inches from my eyes, and I start to suspect she is pretty deeply non-sober. Their kids, on the blanket in front of us, the two-year-old is asleep in the fetal position. The older one, who might be three or also two, I don't know, is looking up at the screen with big eyes, thinking something, probably like, "Do rhinoceri chase people on a frequent basis?"

"Bob?"

Melinda knows my name. This is progress.

"Bob, why do you live here? Like, we like you and all, but I'm just wondering. Like, movie night with a bunch of parents? You're a single guy."

A couple answers occur in my panicked brain. Like, I got a good deal on the house or maybe I could claim it's close to work, but I am pretty sure I told them I was a freelance tech consultant so that might not be a good idea. I go with, "I just needed some space," which is not true, but is imbued with the essence of something true and therefore is a good lie.

It seems to satisfy her. Her face recedes back into the darkness and I sense her settling back into her lawn chair.

I collapse cross-legged in the grass. Everybody else brought a blanket or lawn chairs, but the grass is thick and soft and dry enough, and the movie goes on for as long as we need it to.

"A bunch of parents," she'd said. As I replay the sentence in my head, it stretches and whirs like an old movie reel stretching and whirring. Had she not said "parents," but spat it, like a Roaring Twenties Railroad Baron might spit the word "Chinaman"? Did she hate being reduced to "parents" that much? Hate the weekend nights now spent stretched over green grass instead of a motel mattress? Or maybe had she only over-whispered the word, lowered it so as not to offend all these other parents, our neighbors? Or was there maybe a wink behind it, like she knew, like she knew I was merely hiding here with them while I waited for some terrible something in my past to be forgotten?

The more I replay Melinda's words in my head, the harder they are to hear. Soon, they are gone.

The movie ends. Jacob and Melinda carry their sleeping kids home. I offer to help carry their blankets and lawn chairs, but they say no, they've got it, and disappear into the stream of other families, dispersing into Winegrove.

These people are all in their mid-30's now. Six or eight years older than me, more or less, depending on when they decided to move to the suburbs and have kids. This is me and Mandy in another life. Or maybe me and Danica, if she hadn't been such a psycho.

I pick my way through the park and along dark sidewalks to my home. It is a Friday night and tomorrow, Saturday, I will have to all-nighter and deliver the milk again, so tonight I stay up as late as I want, searching Webworld for stories about goat monsters stalking America's suburbs. I don't find any. I find witches and ghosts and lots of coyotes. I also find a disturbing amount of Suburbanites who swear they see metal tubes zipping through the air, and who believe those tubes to be probes sent by aliens. But I find no rumors of cat-eating monsters with hooves and/or horns.

Eventually, I fall asleep alone.

A couple days later I go to the pound and tell the young woman in tan scrubs at the front desk I want to get a cat.

"What kind of cat?"

"One that doesn't move much."

"Are you open to an adult cat?"

I nod.

"Because a lot of young families want a kitten, so they can play with him or her."

"I don't have a family," I say. "An adult is fine. I'd just like a cat I can, like, lay on the floor with. Watch movies and stuff."

"So indoor cat more than outdoor cat?"

"Indoor, I guess?"

"You care if he has claws?"

"I mean, not really."

"Because if he or she goes outside, it's better if they have their claws."

"I think it's ok if he doesn't have claws."

"You want a boy cat?"

"Either way."

"Because you said he."

"No, um, but either way is fine."

She takes me through a metal door into a row where the cats are kept in exhibits stacked three high. Exhibit is basically a nice word for cage and each one has a steel door with a little square window in it. There must be a zillion exhibits, but she points out three or four in particular. In one, I see a cat I like. He is sleeping, breathing very steadily. He has white fur and a gray face, flat like his nose has been smushed up between his eyes. It is brighter in the exhibit/cage than it is here, the row where I am standing, and I wonder if he, the cat, can see me, wondering this while the woman gets him out and hands him to me and he just sort of drapes there across my folded arms, looking up, wondering only why I disturbed his nap. He weighs about five or four kilo bars of gold.

She tells me he is a Himalayan Cat, and that she thinks he's 11 or 12 years old. She tells me what the price will be, that I have to pay for his shots and neutering, even though they already did all that, and I say that's perfect even though I'm not really paying attention.

I ask if he already has a name and she says not that she knows of. I am planning to call him Dashain, which is a festival in Nepal. And Dashain means hope and they sacrifice goats at this festival, but I don't see any reason to tell her that.

She puts him in a cardboard carrier for the trip home, which I put on the floor of the passenger seat. But after five minutes, I hear the folds of the top of the carrier box scraping against each other and when I look down, I see Dashain's flat face pushing out. I reach down with my right hand and open the box and he climbs out, into the passenger seat, and right over onto my lap. He puts his two front paws up on the driver side door and takes a peek out the window at the Monday day sliding by, and then curls down into my lap.

We stay like that the rest of the drive home.

The afternoon is becoming evening. The streetlights are buzzing and then flickering on. I drive from one scene to the next faster and faster and when I finally drive fast enough, a new movie begins.

There are these videos I watch on Webworld that I'd never admit to having watched. They are videos that help guys be more liked, with titles such as "How to Turn Awkwardness into Charm!" and "How Popular Guys Deal with Rejection!" And when I get home, me and Dashain settle cross-legged on the floor and watch one of these videos together, "How Magnetic Men Approach Women!"

I can't recall how I first approached Mandy or Danica. Or any of the other women I dated. There was often liquor involved so maybe that was it. But I think there was something else too, something I said or a certain way I stood, something that these days I can't or won't remember.

Then again maybe it is just easier to meet people when you are younger. I don't know. I've always been younger than I am.

Dashain sits on my lap, his head pushed into my belly. Maybe he is sleeping, maybe he is ashamed his new best friend is watching video lessons about how to approach women. Either way, it is a good sign that I am not invisible to him.

Chapter 12
Deception

A city day like this, summer turning into late summer, wind blowing hard, I see this leaf in my path being held up in front of me, hanging in place, and I reach out to pluck it out of the air and it turns out it isn't a leaf but a bee struggling to get up above the eddies. Stings me right in the palm of my hand.

This is a problem, because my plan, such as it was, was to go to Kristy Lee's gym over lunch and play basketball, and, if she happened to be there, we could happen to bump into each other, and I could ask her out.

Part of me says this is a newly creepified level of stalking. But is it? What's the difference between doing what I am doing, I reason, and going to a coffee shop where I think the barista is cute and asking her out? There is a difference, I know there is, but I can't name it.

Anyway, it works, because I can't play basketball because my hand is throbbing because a bee stung me in it.

And so I end up running on a treadmill and she, Kristy Lee, gets on the one next to me out of nowhere. I look over, there she is, and the little button is beeping as she accelerates the belt on the treadmill. And right before she puts her earbuds in, she looks over at me and she sees me. And in this moment, I am not invisible. In fact, I am the opposite of invisible. It is like the whole sun has turned its warm, loving attention only on me and I matter.

And I warn myself, this is not real. Kristy Lee is just one of those women who you think you have a special relationship with, when the truth is she just knows how to make everyone she meets feel special.

And then I take a deep breath and say, "You want to know my favorite joke?"

I don't tell her my favorite joke though, the frog one. I tell her a much shorter one, one that is funny mostly because it's so dumb it's endearing. Like, you want to pet the joke on the head just for trying.

And then I say I don't want to interrupt her workout any more than I already have, so how about I take her to dinner sometime. It's so forward and yet so natural. And she says Saturday but I can't Saturday because of milk. And I think maybe in some weird way, me saying no to Saturday makes her like me even more.

We agree on Sunday night.

Chapter 13
Passivity

I stack the boxes and the flats around in the milk delivery car until they are in a perfect order. This is harder than it sounds. The half-gallons are on pallets that are 36 inches deep and 18 inches wide. The gallons are on pallets that are 36 inches deep but 24 inches wide. The cream cheese is in boxes that are 18 inches wide by 18 inches deep by 18 inches high, so they are perfect cubes. And so on and so on. The back of the delivery vehicle is 18 feet deep by eight across. I don't know how high it is, but I am a shade over six feet and I have to stoop down if I don't want my head to bonk the ceiling.

The eggs come in crates that go on a special shelf along the side, I assume because they break so easily.

On the road in the night I am a rectangle inside a box that drives in squares. Everything is orderly until it leads to a place where people live.

I am feeling fairly confident though. I have brought a

baseball hat and also a hoodie and I put my hat on and my hoodie up and figure that if the neighborhood can't agree what they saw on Josie's doorbell cam, whether it was a goat monster or a werewolf or a bigfoot with a cat or a tumbleweed or a package, or whether it was all nothing at all, then they definitely won't be able to identify their milkman as the neighbor they are just now getting to know.

Maybe I am too sure in all of this, because I am not paying attention to the thing I should be paying attention to.

Every home in the hood has a default weekly order. For the first couple weeks, I started each stop by walking up the steps and/or sidewalk to the front door, checking to see if they wanted their default order or if they wanted some other assortment of goods, and then walking back to the truck to get it. Eventually, I realized most people either wanted their default order or they would forget to fill their order sheet out, in which case the default action was to deliver their default order. So it was faster to get out the default order by default, and then if they wanted something different, go back to the van to swap things.

Point is that when I get to the Supperville's house at 3:47 a.m., I come out of the back of the van with one half-gallon of 2% milk, one six pack of bottled water, one half-gallon of orange juice and one pint of half + half in my arms. This takes a bit of concentration to carry without falling down and it is not until I am actually on their front porch that I realize I am not alone. I am the opposite of alone. I am with someone. Dana is sitting there in the darkness, feet tucked up under her on their porch swing.

Dana says, "Morning." My eyes bug right out of my face and I clench all the groceries to my chest. Then her face comes out of the darkness and I can see her see me. Because unfortunately I have become less invisible.

"You… Hi."

"Yeah, hey."

She is wearing just the top half of a set of pajamas. I wonder if Greg Supperville - movie-hosting, catless insurance agent - is asleep in bed and if he is wearing the other half of the PJs, the bottoms.

"You deliver the milk? You're our milkman?"

There is no way I can say no to this, although I very much consider it. Just say, "Nope," and leave. Instead I say, "Look," and then I level with her enough for it not to be a lie exactly. "I don't need to work. I have money. This is just, like, to pass the time. But I, like, don't like people knowing it because then they act weird."

"It is weird."

"Not the job. That's just because I like the night, I like the quiet. I'm working on a screenplay during the day. Or an art project." I'm freestyling now, needlessly embellishing, my half-truth becoming a full-lie. I have to reel it back in. "What I don't want people knowing is that I don't have to work for money."

"If I was rich," she says, "I wouldn't live here."

"Well, but... I'm not rich. I just have some investments

and it's enough I can live off the what do you call it?"

"Passive income?"

"Yeah."

"The interest?"

"Yeah?"

"The residuals?"

"I just don't want anyone to know."

"This is creepy, Rob."

"Bob."

"Right."

And suddenly I am the one creeped out. Dana doesn't seem especially phased by the hooded neighbor she's found with an armful of groceries on her porch. She just seems very sad.

"I'm sorry about your cat," I say, trying casually to change the subject and coming off like a non-empathetic person in doing so. "It was your cat that, like, disappeared or whatever?"

"It was my daughter's cat."

"Is she sad?"

"Is she sad?"

I should shut up now but I say, "Is Greg? How's Greg?"

"How's Greg?"

She's sitting there and I'm realizing there have been a lot of nights I've seen lights on at the Supperville's, shadows behind curtains, people up in the dark. Just never out here, thinking, killing time on the porch like this. Maybe the weather just hadn't been warm enough until tonight.

"You've been talking to people. About us."

I vaguely remember Jacob saying something about spousal swapping, and I shake my head but maybe she sees the penny drop because she says, "By the way, I never thanked you for the party the other night."

"Sure."

"Tell me, Bob the Milkman, would you like to come to one of my parties sometime?"

"Uh, maybe, I guess sure?"

"Oh, but our parties aren't what you may've heard. People say the dumbest things. They tell stories. But there's no wife swapping. There's no naked bodies. No masks or sexual games. In fact, there's only one rule."

"One rule."

"Yes. Everyone has to whisper."

"At your parties?"

"Like this," she says. With one hand she reaches out and covers her WAR cam and then she leans forward, up out of her seat, leaning into me, pushing herself onto tiptoes so her mouth first hovers by my lips and then slowly moves over my cheek. She noses her way inside the hood of my hoodie, nuzzling up to my ear where she stops and I can hear her wet her lips with her tongue. It's like magic, that wetting so loud in my ear and yet impossible for anyone else to ever hear.

This moment is just for me.

Her entire body hovers near mine, not touching me and yet I can feel it pressing on me, her aura or her gravity as sensual as even naked skin might have been. Finally I feel her lips move as she whispers. "Thanks for delivering our milk, Bob. I appreciate you so much."

She settles back down off her tiptoes, tilts away from me, sits all the way down into her swing, and folds her hands in her lap.

Me, I'm frozen. My breath has totally stopped and I'm pretty sure my heart has stopped too.

She smiles a smile so sweet it's evil. She is a drug dealer and she has given me that first taste. "It's amazing, isn't it?"

After a couple seconds a big shudder goes through me, starting at the surface of my skin and moving inward to jumpstart my heart. I suck in a huge breath of air.

"Yeah," I pant doggystyle.

"It doesn't even matter what you say. It's just so intimate. The guys don't whisper too much into each other's ears, of course. I mean, they do at first, but by the end of the night, they're mostly just standing around with their hands in their pockets." She rolls her eyes playfully. "Trying to hide their hard-ons."

"Yeah," I say, still struggling to breathe. "I bet."

"Would you want me to invite you sometime?"

"Totally." I am very emphatic about this.

Dana shifts in her seat, knowing I want absolutely nothing more than to have her whisper in my ear again. But instead she wiggles five fingers at me. "Adios, Bob. Don't let the goat monster get you. And don't worry. Your secret's safe with me."

The rest of my deliveries, I am very careful to make sure no one sees me.

When I get back to Moo Cow, where the sex slave dude had been chained up there now stands a man wearing black jeans and a black jacket. There are warehouses all around and it's not impossible that he works at one of them and now, his car broken down, he's standing by the side of the road in the dark, waiting for some wife, who might work as a waitress at an all night diner, to cruise by, pick him up and drive him back to their little home, somewhere in some ungentrified section of Aspenroot. Except as I drive past him, he looks up at me and by lamplight I can see something is horrifically wrong with the left side of his face. It is too wrinkled to be a burn scar, too warped to be a birthmark. It sort of looks like he might have had a stroke, but it sort of looks like the stroke might have been delivered by the broadside of a shovel. It's safe to say he hasn't been kissed in a whole lot of years, and most likely never will be again.

I try not to stare out my window as I turn past him into the parking lot, but I fail and then I also glance back to make real sure he has two feet. Soon he is just a silhouette in my sideview mirror.

Inside Moo Cow, the teen receptionist is looking out her one tiny window. I worry about her, if she'll have to go to her other receptionist job in the morning. And I wonder what time she leaves Moo Cow and if I should stay till then, just to make sure this half-faced man is gone.

As always, the sun is up before I leave. As always, I ride my bike home, premeditatedly straight streets connecting premeditatedly twisty ones.

Chapter 14
Conversation

This was the question I asked back when I used to be good at dating and got girls like Mandy and Danica:

"What did you do you never got caught for?"

I asked it of all my dates, because it encouraged them to think in secret and sexual ways from the very beginning of the relationship. And sure enough, I can see it lolling about in the back of Kristy Lee's beautiful mind. There must have been many things. A test she cheated on, a boy she cheated on. Salacious stories, simple once but made delicious in the retelling. The sushi restaurant is humming very quietly, maybe only half full on this Sunday night.

When we'd arrived, she told me it's dangerous to eat sushi on Sunday because that's when restaurants are trying to get rid of all the rotting fish they couldn't unload on Friday or Saturday, which are more proper date nights, after all. But when I asked her if she wanted to go somewhere else, she said not to worry about it.

"I don't know. Let me think about it."

"OK."

"What about you?"

"What about me?"

"What did you do you never got caught for?"

"Bad ideas, I guess."

"What kind?"

"The crazy kind. The Bonnie and Clyde kind, but a country club version of Bonnie and Clyde. The idea maybe me and this crazy girl would decide to run away together and never come back."

"What happened?"

"I took the cash instead."

And then she asks, "What was that idea worth?"

And I say, "For me it was somewhere around $800,000."

But she doesn't catch it. Instead she says that was the tagline on SuperMeme's biggest wall, the one all the clients saw the first time they walked into the agency, words painted big in block type.

What's an idea worth?

She nods while she remembers. She runs her fingernail around the edge of the wine glass while nodding and I watch her sexy fingernail, not the nodding.

She says, "I have an idea." She doesn't have to tell me what it is. I lean over and kiss her. That I remember how to do, back from when I was a whole human person. We kiss for a while and drink some more wine and then kiss again.

Her lips taste better with the wine but her tongue tastes better in the spaces in between it.

"I have to admit something," I say.

"Yeah?"

"Before we went out, I was looking you up on Webworld just to make sure you're not, like, crazy."

"Oh no."

"Yeah, and you're the girl from the, you know, you said you worked at SuperMeme just now. And you're famous from the crime a few years ago."

She laughed. "You asked, what did I never get caught for. And it's the exact opposite. I got caught in the biggest, most public way possible, right? I have one quickie and the whole nation knows about it. 'Couple Making Out In Office Escapes Mass Murder.' It was the most embarrassing headline ever."

I don't say anything, like, one way or the other.

She says, "I looked you up, too. All your feeds just said you were taking a break from social. I couldn't find you on any dating apps, either."

I give a shrug that could mean anything.

"I don't like the apps either, but after the Slaughter, I sort of took a break from dating and then I had to get my career back together. Hiring managers would interview me for the novelty of talking with one of the only survivors of a mass shooting, but at the time I was kind of a hot mess. And then next thing you know I'm in my 30s and suddenly the only guys DM'ing me are divorced 45-year-old dudes with tween-age kids."

"You don't look like you're in your 30s," I say.

But she's kind of offended by this and she says, "What's wrong with being in your 30s?"

And I'm like, "Nothing." And part of me wants to scream how Jacob Coral risked his whole career just to chase her and then when that didn't work he married her doppelganger and moved to a house in the suburbs and had babies. And part of me wants to know if it is OK to go back to the part of the story where we were kissing, has that scene passed, did I ruin it? And another part of me just wants to know the question, the answer to which is, "Joe Mead."

"What?"

I realize I said the quiet part loud. "It was... I was just thinking about what you said. 'One of the only survivors.' One was, like... Joe Mead was the security guard?"

"When Jacob went back to New York - Jacob was the other survivor, the one I was, you know what we were doing, the one I was with - anyway, afterwards, I tried to keep in touch with Joe since we were both in Aspenroot, but he was just an odd guy. I hung out with him once after work at this awful bar all the way out on Gilbert called Confluence. I guess that was, like, his place. He must've had this thing for this one girl, this girl Rowan McGregor, who was an assistant in the accounting department. He'd be like, 'No one survived, everyone died, especially Rowan McGregor.' And I'd be like, 'Especially?' And he'd say he meant 'including.' I think he liked her or something? But you know, he was pretty smart. But weird. Just awkward all the time. But he seemed like one of those guys who gets a job as a security guard just so he can carry a gun."

Kristy Lee's great-grandpa had driven a shotgun across state lines. She'd no way of knowing if the old man had even realized he was committing a felony. He was ninety at the time, top of his bald head one big liver spot, white pants on occasion, terrible tennis shoes the only ones that fit his aching feet. And yet she liked to imagine him stopping his car on the Ohio River, where Indiana becomes Kentucky. And she could see him sitting, motor idling, watching the river wash the barges by, hands wrapped to white on the steering wheel, considering that this thing he was about to do, once done, could never be undone. Never again could he be just a mild-mannered retired bridge architect. He'd be a felon on the run. A one deep breath and the crossing over the Ohio River also a crossing into some new self, a commitment to a criminal way of life. She imagined him on the bridge pushing the pedal hard, speeding into America.

That shotgun itself had been his, 1920-ish. In that place and at that time, a dad bought his eight-year-old a bird gun to carry into the woods. When it'd arrived in her keeping, Kristy Lee'd had no idea if it was functional or even loaded. She'd taken it to a gunsmith, she claimed, and she said she told that gunsmith to remove the firing pin or the spark plug or whatever it was that made shotguns go bang. And once that was done, she'd hung it simply as art and history on the wall. Looking at it, she felt connected in some small way, part of a long line of McIllvinneys. And also she had some idea some man might break into her apartment some night and she'd brandish her great grandpa's gun knowing it'd never fire and the intruder would fear her and run away. But mostly, she kept the shotgun for another reason, which was it'd been given to her and she had a hard time parting with things.

That's the story she told me.

And, after we have sex, I eye that weapon for a time. What is it about me and girls who have shotguns? Does two count as a trend?

I say, "Hey, look, it's Chekhov's gun."

"What's Chekhov's gun?"

"Chekhov was this Russian writer. And he had this thing about not showing the audience, he was a playwright, not showing them anything that didn't have a role in the story. So if you show the audience a gun in the first act of a play, at some point in the third act you have to fire it."

She nods, slowly. "I think I could. Fire a gun. You know. If I had to."

"Do you think about it much, The Super Slaughter?"

"I'm not sure," she says and stretches out on the bed till her fingertips hit her golden satin headboard and her toes just almost reach the golden metal footboard. "I have a terribly inconsistent memory. Most of my life, all my childhood... I don't know why but I can't recall it. Things I did yesterday I forget. Songs and pictures hold nothing for me. But when I hold things, everything I've ever done with those things in my hands comes back to me. And with the Super Slaughter, it was like it didn't even happen. I threw away the dress and Jacob, he airplaned away. And then I had nothing to touch and I never even felt bad. Not really. I said I did because you're supposed to, all those people die, you're supposed to be sad. But I couldn't really remember it, even. Like it happened far away. And when Jacob came back a couple times, we tried to date. And we tried. We had one date at this bar, it was raining. And we tried but when we kissed, it all came back. All those people I knew. All their blood."

She says she has to go to work in the morning so I have to leave. She also says she usually doesn't do this having-sex thing on the first date. Is this an authentic statement or do I just want it to be an authentic statement? The latter, probably. She is a confident adult, a woman in her 30's. She probably has sex on all her first dates, just to see if the guy is worth having a second date with. She doesn't have time to waste time.

Personally I go home and sleep a bit and then throw a tennis ball at the ceiling. Dashain finds me and sits on my carpet watching. Just two friends, breathing the same air.

After a couple hours of this, I get out my laptop, do some Webworlding, and find an article in an ad industry trade pub that isn't hidden behind a firewall.

"What's an idea worth?" The headline says, and the

copy reads:

"The advertising industry suffered an incalculable blow to one of its freshest agencies over the holidays. The mass shooting at the SuperMeme/Aspenroot holiday party was a tragedy of Shakespearean proportions. And the industry now wonders if SuperMeme will shutter its doors forever. Founded just a few years ago, SuperMeme made no attempt to hide its ambition to change the business model of the entire advertising industry. In fact, many competitors griped that the most creative thing it ever produced was its billing structure, which charged clients not for the hours employees worked, but for the subjective quality of their ideas. This exciting, even revolutionary process won SuperMeme a lot of new business pitches with clients hungry for new compensation arrangements. But it also set SuperMeme up for controversy, as those same clients demanded transparency, asking to see the hours and the senior staffers behind the ideas - hours and senior staffers SuperMeme was often unable to produce. 'Give them credit,' said Gore Baker, CEO of Gore Baker. 'They're at least trying to innovate. Right now, we're sending the rest of their staff and all of their families our condolences.' As of yet, there's no word if SuperMeme's other offices will continue operation, or shutter their doors forever in the wake of this incomprehensible tragedy."

I shut my laptop and look at Dashain and ask him, "What's an idea worth?"

He opens one eye and looks at me. It doesn't look like

he cares or it looks like his idea is we ought to take a nap.

I don't really feel like taking a nap though. So I text Jacob, see what he is up to this Monday evening, and meet him on his porch shortly thereafter. And I sit there and wonder if he can smell the love-of-his-life's scent still smeared over me, because I can. And maybe he can, but only subconsciously, because we sit there in the summer and guzzle gin fizzes and he finally tells me the true story of their second and third dates.

Chapter 15
The Story of the Luckiest Lovers

"I was in Aspenroot on a shoot, perhaps a year and some months after the Super Slaughter, the completion of which was celebrated with a wrap party, the cost of which was directly proportional to the budget allotted to the commercial production. This production was for the launch of a new pickup truck and it'd been big enough to fly sundry agency-folk and multiple clients into Aspenroot. So you better bet the wrap party warranted belly dancers and hors d'oevres on steel trays.

"Almaza Pilsners became Washington Apples and Flaming B52's which became Poudre Canyon Dropoffs which became, well, who could possibly remember? And I had dressed for the occasion. I wore olive leather shoes with just enough tread to grip the dance floor and a black shirt underneath my charcoal jacket so I could easily hide spills and errant sweat. I danced and drank and may have even kissed or been kissed. But the foggier my vision and the dimmer the lights, the clearer and brighter the memory of Kristy Lee McIllvinney became. And when I awoke in my hotel bed – alone and warm, slightly hungover and very hungry – all I saw was the lack of her. The empty space on the vanilla sheets; the undented 300 thread count cotton sateen pillowcase.

"The production calendar left two days between the end of the shoot and the beginning of the edit. And while I was nominally working remotely – balancing emails and conference calls with the hours on set – I found that the less accessible I was, the harder everyone assumed I was working. And so that morning I showered and dressed in a pair of raw denim jeans with honeycombs behind my knees and hige fades in the crotch, a v-neck t-shirt that dipped just enough to show my collarbone, and a chunky cardigan with a patch in the right elbow. I brushed my teeth and tousled my hair, picked up my phone and a paperback I had only the barest intention of reading, and headed towards the hotel lobby for coffee and a pass through the breakfast buffet.

"How early was too early to send the text? Not before ten, certainly. But the top of the hour seemed obvious and therefore needy, so I settled on fourteen after. I walked out of the hotel lobby and found a bench somewhere along some sidewalk, where I watched valets park cars and couples walk past, arms already full of pink paper shopping bags badged with cursive logos. At last I typed and sent the word, 'Hi.' I waited and waited and in that time the sun seemed to shine solely on Aspenroot. It played across my face and made my cardigan untenably hot until I stripped it off and felt the light on my pale arms. And finally my phone vibrated, and when it did I suddenly realized how hard I had been clutching it, how white my knuckles had turned. I looked at the message and it said, 'Hi, sailor.'

"My heart was filled with joy but there was something else too, a feeling I don't think any woman could possibly understand. A dam burst and an ancient river flooded my bloodstream, spreading outward until my skin felt swollen, angry, jumpy and tender as the blood pressed outward from my heart. And I breathed deep, my senses raw, able to taste salt in the air even here, 1,000 miles from any shore. I wanted to write, 'Busy?' or 'What's up' or 'Got time for coffee?' But what my thumb tapped and sent was, 'I'm in Aspenroot. How soon can I see you?' And she sent back, 'Now.' And then, seconds later, an address. And I did not even respond. I used my phone to call a car and gave the driver the address and as the car pulled away from the curb, I caught myself panting and thought myself pathetic but did not care.

"I crashed through the door and caught Kristy Lee around the waist. We did not speak. We kissed only on the neck and on each other's cheeks and along our jawlines. And then it was the Super Slaughter all over again, Kristy Lee's skirt around her waist and my pants around my ankles as I tried to find the fastest way into her. And only after I'd entered her did I pause and think, 'O world! O life! O time!

On whose last steps I climb, trembling at that where I had stood before; when will return the glory of your prime? No more – Oh, never more.' I knew I had not written those words but could not name their source. And when I tried to crawl inside my mind and find the page from whence they'd come, I felt Kristy Lee buck insistently against me, reminding me that my attention belonged only here and now and on her, that the Princess of Aspenroot both demanded and deserved my very best efforts.

"As I began to move, she said, 'Jesus fuck, I feel so alive.'

"It was over within moments, and there was nothing skillful or acrobatic about it. In fact, it was as if we were cheating death again, as if we were still locked in that office room as we had been more than a year before. And when it was over we were surprised and overjoyed to realize the afternoon stretched before us like a country highway. So much road to travel, but only one direction it could possibly lead.

"Kristy Lee smoothed her skirt and said – panted, really – 'Do you want a drink. Or coffee. Or anything?' She was trembling, her chin buried down, her eyes angled up. She could have been a shamed puppy looking up at its master or a prizefighter stepping into the ring – it was simply impossible to tell which. I pulled up my pants and zipped them. It seemed the thing to do. I sat on her soft emerald couch amongst a dozen pillows.

"I flew back to New York a couple days later. But I

knew. I had to move to Aspenroot. I had to be here. Near her.

"The luckiest lovers in the world would not meet again for two years, but when we did, it was as if heaven'd determined to deliver unto us the most romantic afternoon a man and a woman had ever seen. Over the course of several text messages and one whispered call, we'd arranged to rendezvous on a sidewalk outside a bar somewhere in the Art District. The sun was most likely halfway between the apex and the horizon, but no one knew for sure because it'd been blotted out by gray mountain clouds and a rainstorm welling out there, gathering force on top of the divide.

"The street itself was filled with antique furniture stores and costume jewelers, and I stood at the door of the only bar around, waiting ever so patiently. (Or at least looking like I hadn't a care in the world.) I did not once tap at my phone or look at my little black book. I kept my hands in my pockets, except when I had to remove one to brush back the thick locks of curly brown hair that sometimes spilled carelessly into my eyes.

"She came skipping up the street in a poodle skirt and a 'do out of the Fifties, as retro glam was the favored flavor among starlets that spring. And she stopped and stood at a spot just a little too far away. And I lifted myself from the wall I'd been leaning against and I stood before her, too. And what we both felt was joy and sparkles, the premonition our lives had just gotten a whole lot more interesting. But what we both said was, 'Hi.'

"I thumbed over my right shoulder. 'I'm sorry, the reviews said it was good, but the bar, it's closed.'

"'Oh!' she replied. She cupped her hands over her eyes (careful not to muss her eyelashes!) and leaned against the pane. 'It looks very cool inside. Oh, but someone is coming!'

"And like that, the door swung open and a proprietor carrying a washcloth and wearing an apron stated, 'I'm not open yet.'

"'It's fine,' I said, not-quite-so-young and presumptive as I once was. 'We just were trying to find a place to have a drink. Is there somewhere else around?'

"The proprietor looked at us two. 'Just a drink? No food? Because the kitchen isn't up yet.'

"'Just a drink, but you don't have to open just for us.'

"'Ah, it's fine.' The man waved us in. And behind us, he locked the door.

"He mixed us cocktails – a Mary Pickford for the lady, a Gin Rickey for you, good sir – and then retired to the kitchen, leaving us alone.

"Outside, the clouds reached the city and the air grew heavy, a fine mist that dampened the windows of the bar. But to us, it almost looked like the glass had fogged over not because of the mist outside, but from our own wet breath.

"Kristy Lee tasted her drink, careful to make sure I was watching as she set her lips softly upon the rim of her glass. And then she asked, 'So?'

"'So,' I agreed. 'Here we are.'

"'It's good to see you again.'

"'You're out of the ad game?'

"'I'm doing fashion. I write at a fashion magazine and I blog. But mostly I'm a buyer. I buy for Cash Register.'

"'Sounds fun.'

"'It's not any easier, if that's what you're thinking. People in advertising think they have it so hard. But it's the same anywhere you go. You're working fifty hours a week or you're not working.'

"'Fifty's all?'

"'Let's not play the martyr game. Everyone from New York is so convinced they're keeping America afloat, they all work eighty hours a week and simply must do as much coke as possible to keep up. Yawn. It's hard everywhere you go. Personally, I'm stressed so often stress is beginning to bore me. You're still slaving away?'

"I nodded, but how could I ever be expected to explain it? Day after day after day on end, blender mornings dissolved into high-five nights. Steadying coffees at sunrise bled into smashing highballs come sunset. The game was a train and I had both feet on it, though I had no idea where it would take me. 'Yeah, I left SuperMeme though. I told them it was because of, because of, you know. But really, I just wanted to move on. I worked at H/T for awhile as a senior, and got offered this ACD gig at MOUNTAIN right when they won Cannes so that seemed like a good move. But I always liked Aspenroot, so when a job opened up at a place here, I took it.'

"She stopped. She stiffened. She said, 'You're in Aspenroot? To live?'

"'I'm moving here. Next month. Permanently.'

"The world held its breath and Kristy Lee looked at me, some war upon her face.

"'And?' she whispered.

"'And,' I surrendered, 'I'm sure it'll be like you said. It's the same everywhere you go. It's a lot of hours, mostly people skills, whoever gets the client to laugh at their stuff wins. Advertising has been good to me. But come on. I make a living convincing people to buy things they don't need. It's amazing they pay me a buck and a quarter to do this job.'

"'I bet you're a whiz at salary negotiations.'

"'I get what the market will bear.'

"By this point, our rocks glasses were practically licked dry. The proprietor came back out and asked if we wanted another. We nodded hard yeses.

"The man served us and walked away. And we swiveled to face each other in our stools and there was a moment when our eyes met and our mouths stopped making sounds. The rain had become a machine gun on the streets and the sidewalks and most of all the windowpanes, as loud as all of Christopher Gouldberg's weapons combined. I leaned to her, lips opening just a bit, but she turned her cheek and said, 'I don't know. Can we just?'

"I pulled back, a gentleman after all. But for me it was

too late, the scent of her was in my lungs. I remembered what it'd been to be inside her, all wetness and abandon. And at that moment, I would have traded my career and my clothes and maybe my life for a single flutter of her eyelashes.

"We continued to talk. But we were both students of the game. We kept our body posture open and our heads nodding almost imperceptibly up and down. And we both made eye contact as a matter of practice and habit, always seeking to develop and demonstrate empathy. But together, the unintended consequence was that we found ourselves never breaking away from one another, not even for a moment. Her spritely blue eyes, my warm chocolate ones. They locked and they held as we drank and talked and drank and talked. And nature was stronger than either of us. All that eye contact made us vulnerable, opened our souls, left our loves stripped bare for the other to go spelunking across.

"The proprietor returned to ask if we needed a third and then suggested, 'Listen, here's the bottle. You just help yourselves.' And then he disappeared back into the kitchen and outside this empty, locked bar, the clouds had gathered energy from some distant ocean and carried it over the mountains and now were letting loose cannons of thunder, spears of lightning, bullets of rain.

"'You seem like you've lost your passion for it?'

"I shrugged.

"'You've never wanted to try the writing thing?

Screenplays or something?'

"'Ads are what they pay me for.'

"'No,' she shook her sage head, knowing something about me I didn't even know about myself. 'It's not the money with you.'

"'It's not?'

"'No, it's me. Not just me, but girls like me. What agency doesn't have a dozen skinny blondes running around? The industry attracts them. If you were a writer-writer, you'd have to spend your days alone in a café somewhere, begging some hippie barista to comp your espressos.'

"I didn't want to admit it. I rolled my eyes. 'You don't think being a screenwriter or something'd be just as good? Lot of beautiful women in Hollywood.'

"'You hear the joke about the starlet so dumb she slept with the writer? No, in Hollywood, writers are just the director's fifteenth most important assistant. But in ad agencies, writers are stars, and you get to spend all day with all these cute account girls, all dressed up all the time. The interns probably think you're so cool.'

"'Maybe. But even interns' drinks cost money. New York was a pricey town.'

"She picked up her glass, drained it and showed me the emptiness. 'I'm not a whore. If that's what you think.'

"'No, I don't think you're a whore. To be a whore, you have to be able to sell stuff. And the better salesperson here is me.'

"'So sell it. Why should we try to start seeing each other, after all this time?'

"'I don't have to.'

"'No?'

"'I don't, because in your marketing school, the one got you the SuperMeme internship in the first place, they probably taught you about the Theory of Natural Markets.'

"'Marketing 101. We're sitting here in this bar, locked in, with that rainstorm outside, and you're trying to seduce me by lecturing me about Marketing 101.'

"'The Theory of Natural Markets states that when you're selling something, you already know people who want to buy it. They like you, you like the same things, the sale becomes as easy as a handshake.'

"'I remember the theory.'

"'People have a natural market too. Just by virtue of being in the same place at the same time, we already know we have the same goals. That night, think about how hard you had to work, just to get in that room. How much effort you put into dressing the way you did. Just by virtue of standing next to each other, we already knew we valued the same things, had succeeded at a job the other person respected. You knew you wanted me before you met me. Selling was as easy as saying hello.'

"The princess once-in-lavender looked down into her glass and saw a woman reflected back. She said, 'Are we still in each other's natural market?'

"And I, the former Duke of New York, said, 'I hope

so.'

"I tried to kiss her again, and again she demurred. Lifted a hand to her neck. Said she needed to use the ladies room. When she came back minutes later she surveyed the wreckage of two hours of flirting and drinking and talking about real things. We'd drank all of one bottle, much of a second and raided the back bar for bitters and orange peels. We had no idea what we owed. No clue where the proprietor even'd disappeared to. I laid $100 cash on the counter and we walked arm-in-arm into the rain.

"It hit us hard, more a tidal wave than a shower, pasting our hair to our cheeks, turning her mascara into body paint and flattening my collar against my shoulders. Through the mountains, down a hill and across the creeks and the grasslands, the rain was washing Aspenroot in steel gray, a hail of bullets that tore leaves from branches and pockmarked potholes.

"She looped her arm into mine, ignoring the stinging on her skin, and said, 'Walk me to my car?'

"I nodded. What else could I do? What could any man do?

"It was only a couple blocks away. When we got there she looked at me and asked, 'You remember that night? I was wondering, you remember if you even knew my name before we…'

"I smiled. 'Probably. Your first name anyway.'

"She stepped back and extended her arm, offering me her hand as she said, 'My name is Kristy Lee McIllvinney.'

"I took her sweet hand in mine. Her skin was so smooth and pink, her fingers so long with fingernails painted the most unassuming shade of peach. Drops of rain slid rolling off them and I had an urge to kneel underneath, drink the water that dripped off her, swallow everything that had ever touched the skin of the Princess of Lavender, Aspenroot and my soul, Kristy Lee McIllvinney. I steadied my heart, brought her hand to my lips, looked up at her with my broody Iberian eyes and slayed her girlish hesitancy dead. 'Kristy Lee, my name is Jacob Coral. It was my privilege to buy your drinks this afternoon.'

"She retrieved her hand, ran the fingers over my cheek and then jumped into me with her whole body, kissed me, opening her lips and searching for my tongue with the tip of her own. We kissed until our clothes soaked through to our skin. And then we kissed some more until Kristy Lee's makeup had washed down her chin and her neck and been swept away into the roiling rivers that rumbled through the gutters of the biggest city in the world. Waters flowed from her mouth. Waters fell from the sky. But as she pulled away from me, away into her car, I realized I'd tasted something else.

"Salt.

"She swerved and turned the corner and as she did I fell to my knees, I pitched onto my palms, I leaned into the gutter, my mouth convulsing, my throat wrenching, my heart ballooning as my body tried in vain to rid itself of the tears of Kristy Lee McIllvinney."

Jacob took a deep breath and said, "Anyway, that was the last time I saw her."

Jacob lolled in his porch swing and I played their second and last dates over and over in my mind until they had a soundtrack, until they had an audience, until said audience was sobbing into its popcorn.

I left Jacob's home and on the sidewalk, somewhere between his house and mine there was a little girl, princess dress muddy, face ruddy with tears, calling out, calling out for a lost cat.

Chapter 16
Infiniteness

I tried to wait multiple days to see Kristy Lee, because I didn't want her to think I was needy or didn't have a life of my own, goals and stuff that women typically like men to have.

I let Monday, Tuesday and Wednesday come and go. Hung out with Dashain, who could really hang out, like do absolutely nothing for hours on end and make it seem like that was the awesomest plan ever. I went and bought him some cat things. Like a scratching post that he sniffed once or twice and then ignored. And a bouncy feather on the end of an elastic string. The package for this showed a cat pawing at the feather playfully, but Dashain just looked at it like it was disturbing his nap. He really was the perfect cat for me, in this life-chapter, anyway.

I also went and shot hoops for an hour a day or so. I rode the 888x in circles, sometimes without even ever getting off to see if I was being followed. And lo and behold, one day someone sat next to me. It was an Asian guy in a tan jacket and he never looked at me the whole time until, at last, he went to get off and when he stood up, I saw he did look at me and I saw he had this wrist band tattoo, which was fine and was probably just a thing he got way back whenever he was in college and probably totally regretted now. The tattoo was just infinity loops around and around, little figure eights set end to end, each one infinite in its own way, connecting just at the tips to make it even more infinite, a series of infinities linked together.

Eventually, Thursday, I sent Kristy Lee a text and I tried not to overthink it, but I didn't have a lot else to do so maybe it was too formal or it felt artificial, inauthentic. But in any case, she didn't respond. I checked in on her social feeds, but they were dark and she didn't seem to ever have posted much personal stuff anyway, just work stuff, stuff that was about her career. So it wasn't like the fact she didn't post for a couple days was strange.

I went to her gym the next Monday and hung out for several hours, hoping she'd pop in but she didn't. I worked out and then went and got a smoothie and then I worked out again, taking my time between sets. Eventually I went home and was very sore the next day.

A couple days later I called her work, planning to hang up if she answered. But she didn't. I got voicemail, so I hit zero for the Cash Register (the business, not the building) receptionist but that stranger just inserted me back into voicemail. I didn't leave a message, obviously.

And thus several days dripped by, during which another weird thing happened.

Dashain was pretty close to unphasable, as in loud noises, lights coming on, nothing bothered him. Annoyed him, maybe. Woke him up and interrupted his basically 24-hour nap. But one night he stiffened, pounced up onto his cat haunches, dug his clawless cat paws into my bedsheets and rotated his two stubby cat ears towards my open window. It was very much the first time I'd ever seen him do anything like that. I reached out my hand and tried to pet him, and through his skin I could feel his spine arched so stiff and hard it was like he had no skin and no fur and was basically just a skeleton.

I got out of bed and looked at my phone. It was 2:42 a.m. and the light from my phone opened my irises, made the room around me and the night outside my window seem even darker than they'd seemed just a minute ago. There was a push notification on my homescreen, asking me if I wanted Webworld to show me ads for WAR cameras. And then I heard it too, the thing that Dashain had heard, the snuffling sound of something breathing heavy, some big something shuffling outside my window.

There's open space not too far from Winegrove, with a bike path paved through it and I know there are foxes and snakes out there, because sometimes at night they go through the hood eating mice, which makes them straight up suburban heroes, as far as all the gardening moms are concerned. But whatever made this noise was way bigger than a fox, or else was a fox with bronchitis.

I looked down out of the window and saw just shadows but one of those shadows was moving and whatever it was, was vertical. It was a one-legged man or a half-faced man. Or a goat monster.

Whatever it was I thought I saw, it didn't look up, didn't acknowledge me staring down out of my window. It slipped around the corner of my house and within a second or two, I was wondering if it could have just been the distorted shadow of something else, something smaller, an owl above or a lost dog below.

And then the pain came and it was like nothing I had ever experienced before. It was like all my neighbors, all these people to whom I was no longer invisible, Jacob and Melinda and Mindy and her husband (whose name I still didn't know) and Josie and Josh and Greg and Dana Supperville too, like all of them placed their flattened palms on my chest and behind me, the walls of my barren home held me fast, crown molding fingering into my spine and fireplace mantles digging at my neck. And all those friendly people all at once just *pressed*.

My throat was too tight to vomit.

My ribs were too tight to breathe.

The dark room got smaller and smaller behind me as I stared out that window at a space where nothing was, maybe nothing ever was.

I fell backwards into bed. There, Dashain was already

asleep.

I wondered how he knew he was safe in my home, or, rather, why he believed he was safe in my home, and, too, why I believed it.

When I woke up the next morning, I looked at my phone and got served a new ad, "Get the NEW Webworld WAR 2 - The first WAR cam designed to sync directly to your Webworld Data Drawers!"

Next evening, there is a knock at my door. More like a banging. Urgent. I pick Dashain up off my thighs and set him down on the floor beside us and he meows low at me, irritated he is losing his bellywarmer, and then he curls up to go back to sleep.

At the door, it's Jacob and evening is behind him, all motionless aqua-purple sky, one color, like Winegrove has been bathed in alpenglow. He has got a look I haven't seen yet, not grimly resigned, not languidly high, not holding court and telling stories. This is something else entirely. This is something as insane as utter joy.

"Bob, dude, you gotta see this."

Two blocks in some direction and another three to the left there's a sizable crowd in front of a house that normally gets a dozen eggs and a gallon of skim milk weekly and apple juice once or twice a month. The house has a riot of flowers outside and they are being trampled by a riot of suburban moms and dads and there's a woman on the porch screaming at them, like, "Get off the flowers."

And Josie is also on the porch screaming, "I told you

so!"

And someone else, a guy, mostly bald, shouts back, "But you said hooves! Goat monster! You said hooves!"

"That's your argument, Basil? I told you there was a cat-eating monster and you're mad because I said it had hooves when actually it has claws?"

"There's not a monster, Josie."

"Maybe it has hooves on its back legs and claws on its front legs."

And the woman who was yelling about the flowers is standing close enough to the bald guy that I assume they are married and she stops yelling about the flowers long enough to reason, "Well, *something* took our cat."

Someone in the lawn says, "You've had your turn, let me see." And they grab for a phone that's in someone else's hands. And now three or four actual adults are fighting over the phone to find out who gets to see the stream from the bald-man and flower-wife couple's WAR cam next. And the flower-wife is yelling, "Get off the flowers" again. And she leans out into the lawn, balancing one hand on what's left of her porch railing carefully because most of it has been ripped away, wood splintered outward into the flowerbeds. And the wood slats at the edge of the porch, they also have been ripped away. And on the pillars that hold them up there are claw marks, like a full grown bengal tiger had climbed up to the very top of them and then got dragged down against his will.

The bald guy and Josie are still debating.

"It was a coyote, Josie."

"A coyote? You know how stupid that sounds?"

"Compared to 'goat monster'?"

"A coyote tore the wood railing off your porch to get to your cat?"

"There's no such thing as a goat monster!"

Two grown men are now punching each other, fighting over who gets to see the bald-man-and-flower-wife couple's phone next.

The people who saw it last are now in an argument, this argument being about whether what they'd watched was a werewolf or the spontaneous combustion of the fence.

Someone says someone ought to go get Simon.

"Who's Simon?"

Jacob is shocked by this question from someone who ought to know better, me. "Your next-door neighbor, Simon? He's a prosecutor, or a cop or a justice department agent or something. Dude, he was at your party, dude? But like, is he going to arrest these people? What do they think he's going to do?"

Simon, I note. Mindy's husband's name is Simon.

Jacob's eyes are very wild. He looks like he's about to laugh and then he is laughing, just giggling to himself.

"This whole thing, man. What a crock of shit," he says.

"Crazy," I say.

"They've got us believing things so hard, we can't believe anything else, even when we see it with our own eyes."

"Did you see the phone?" I ask.

"Oh sure."

"What was it?"

"It was very obviously an alien tractor beam. It shot down from the sky, got the cat in its gravitational vortex, and pulled it up so hard the poor thing went through the fence on its way up to space."

He is laughing so hard. Is he laughing at me or near me? I can't tell. Meanwhile, the bald man's wife is chasing the man who now has the phone through what's left of her flower patch, screeching how she needs it, her phone, back.

Chapter 17
Subjectivity

Friday I catch the 888x and pawn one of the diamonds in a pawn shop in Aspenroot. I do this whenever I run out of cash. Today I visit a pawn shop named Pwn It All.

"What's a diamond worth?"

"Here, whatever I say it is."

"What do you say it is?"

This pawnbroker puts the diamond on a little black leather pad and looks at it through a magnifying glass and then says that today and to him this diamond is worth $8,000 and I have no way of knowing. It's subjective. Diamonds are worth what people will pay. This particular stone is probably worth more than $8,000 to someone else, but how much is it worth to someone who won't care too much about its provenance? That's the main thing. If they ask, I always just say something like, "She said 'no,'" and the man behind the glass counter - it's always a man and it's always a glass counter - always lets it go at that. But this guy doesn't even ask.

I haven't tried to sell the eight gold bars. I like playing dominoes with them too much.

And something occurs to me. It occurs to me I could claim this man, the pawn shopkeep across from me, in his shirtsleeves and with his magnifying glass, for one diamond paid me $8,000 plus a gold bar. And no one would know I was lying. Because the value of a diamond is subjective. It's worth what some human is willing to give you for it.

While he is getting my money and my receipt, which I will throw away, I stroll around the pawn shop. There is a camera tripod leaning in a corner, with an attachment on the top, a clamp to hold a cell phone. I pick it up and collapse the legs and it's easily compact enough in this state to slide into my backpack. There is a price tag on it that says it is $24. When the guy comes back I say I'll give him $20 for it and he tells me I can just take it. Apparently, the profit he made off my diamond put him in a good mood.

And then he asks something embarrassing:

"She say 'no' again?"

Apparently, I have been to Pwn It All before.

The man isn't really looking at me. He's looking down at a paper receipt or something and instead of replying, which would be hard because I have no reply, I just head out the door, which makes a little chiming sound as it shuts behind me.

Eight grand is a good stack of cash, but in hundreds it doesn't weigh much. I slip it and my new phone tripod into my backpack and walk through afternoon towards Cash Register (the building and also the business).

Girls ghost guys all the time. And I knew this. And honestly, while I felt terribly worried, I wasn't terribly worried about Kristy Lee ghosting me. I mean, I liked her, but it wasn't like I thought we were going to have this great relationship and get married and have babies. For one thing, I was basically in a self-imposed witness protection program. But something was worrying me and I couldn't figure out what, maybe something serious or maybe just a little nagging voice warning me that maybe I'd become invisible again.

I knew going to Kristy Lee's work was a nuclear option. She knew me as this guy she met at her gym, and seeing me at her office would require a lie the scope of which I was unprepared for. My only hope was I could hunker down with my phone and a croissant and a coffee and she'd walk right by me, just like she had that first day. I didn't plan to talk to her and if I saw her, I didn't plan to do anything but stop worrying about her and move on with my life.

And this seems like a good plan, a good way to spend this afternoon into evening time. But there is a fatal flaw in my plan. The teenager receptionist person from Moo Cow.

She sees me come in the rotating doors and I have the urge to just keep rotating, rotating back out onto the sidewalk, but it is too late, she's very obviously seen me. She is looking right at me, like she's been expecting me. But of course she is looking at me because what else would a girl do, who is sitting at the info desk in a very large office building in the middle of a quiet summer afternoon? Like, of course she is going to look up at the rotating door to see who is going to rotate out of it.

To my right, a security guard is looking too. And to my left, the coffee stand barista person is also looking. They are all looking at me.

At least, I think, I'm not currently invisible. Which normally would be considered progress, but maybe not today.

The security guard decides I'm no threat and looks back down at whatever security guards have on their desks. And the barista rightly assumes that if I want coffee I'll come over in due time, and she looks away too.

But the receptionist info desk girl does not look away. She smirks. And as if the smirk isn't demeaning enough, she points one long pointer finger at me and cocks her thumb, and, snap, shoots me.

For a sec, I just stand there like an idiot, as if I really have been shot. But then she stops looking at me, dismisses me with her eyelashes, goes back to whatever she's been doing to kill time. And there are just the four of us, all in this massive atrium space, none of us looking at each other even a little.

I buy a paperback and also a coffee from the coffee stand and I pick a soft low chair off to the side where I can see the doors rotating out and the escalator rotating up and at its, the escalator's, top I can see the elevator bays and to their left the hallway going back into the mezzanine level of offices. The dark, cold, quiet, breathing hallway.

And the atrium of the building goes from white-blue to gold and gets golder as the sun drops westward across the city street outside.

The Friday exodus starts with a laugh, two people, a man and woman, at 4:40 p.m. coming down the escalator together and walking click-clack across the atrium and whoosh out the door. And then there are four more and then eight, some of them in suits and pantsuits and some not, some in skirts or jeans, a couple even in shorts. All flooding out of all these arteries, spilling out of all the mezzanine elevators and onto that one escalator. I try to conceal half my face with the paperback and half my face with my paper cup and I peek between them, watching the escalator for Kristy Lee.

The floors above are packed with commuters making their escape and they spread out across the atrium like a river meeting the ocean. But the escalator is a funnel on which they can't stand more than two or maybe three deep and no one can really walk either, not without bowling each other over. And so I really stare at just that escalator. And since my vision is so locked in on it, the escalator, the crowd right in front of me is soft and fuzzy, out of focus.

I am staring over blurry heads, peeking around necks and then, somewhere in the middle distance, standing bone still, there is a man wearing an all-white mask, or rather, a person wearing the all-white mask of a man.

The mask has a smile. The mask has a mustache and an imperial-cut beard running down the chin. I have seen this mask before, I realize, in news reports of the riots in New York maybe a decade back.

This person, it has to be a man, is standing square to me, frozen in the middle of the chaos. He is definitely seeing me. He is tilting his mask-chin to the side as he considers me.

Is anyone else seeing this? They don't seem to. There seems to be me on one side of the atrium and a masked man in its center and, flowing around him like he is a rock in a river, there are thousands of people pushing past, pushing from the mouth of the escalator to the revolving front doors, heads down, watching their feet, watching their phones, oblivious to us both.

And then there is a giant wave of people, a sweeping of humanity across the floor, and when it subsides, the human in the mask is gone.

And then more people are gone and more and more and then by about 7:30 p.m., there are none left. Everyone has gone. The coffee seller throws a cover over her coffee stand and she starts walking and the security guard gets up and slides a big cop flashlight through a ring on his belt and he starts walking and by 8:00 p.m. me and the teenage receptionist are the only people in the atrium of Cash Register, the building.

She stands up and raps a folder of papers on the desk

to get everything aligned, leaves her post, takes a smart 180-degree turn to the base of the escalator and then, right before she steps on, she looks all the way across the atrium and cocks an eyebrow at me, me sitting alone with cold coffee and a terrible book in this cavernous office building in which I've never worked.

I get up with full hands and follow her.

At Moo Cow, I think, I've never seen her in anything but a hoodie and jeans or a hoodie and joggers. But here, in this place, she wears a smart white shirt tucked into a gray skirt just a couple inches too short to be called professional and riding up the escalator several steps behind her, I can see her thighs and around one thigh I can see the ring of a tattoo, infinity symbols looping one into the next into the next.

Maybe it's a tattoo or maybe she'd just got bored, sitting at her desk all day, bleary-eyed from working two jobs, and so maybe she'd started doodling on her thigh with a black ballpoint pen.

But maybe not.

I think about how the guy on the bus had the same tattoo and suddenly my stomach starts to feel like I had too much to drink last night and my breathing starts getting ragged and I'm not able to concentrate on much except putting one foot in front of the other, hypnotized by that hint of infinity-on-thigh.

The receptionist gets off the escalator, strides past the mezzanine elevator bays, and disappears into the mouth of the hallway where I'd hid from Kristy Lee a few days before. I rush to catch up and by the time I reach the hallway, she has disappeared into its darkness.

I step out of the light and start to feel my way after her.

Beneath my feet there's carpet, not loop carpet but a thick navy shag that makes it feel like I am walking on a trampoline, each step I take propelling me a little farther, a little faster.

My eyes start to adjust, and up ahead, I see her sliding her way down the hallway, taking her time, her heels sinking into the carpet, her hips swaying side to side with each step, making a hypnotic little infinity loop of their own. And I am thinking, don't you have to be 18 to get a tattoo? And so maybe she isn't as young as I thought?

Cash Register must sublet the mezzanine level of offices out, because there are strange names on every heavy frosted glass door. Stuudup Protoman. Gavel & Cencik. Constance Battlesby. All names, only names. No indication of who does what or why. Just name after name as I walk and finally, in this finite real world, we reach the end of the hallway, where I find that, deep in the caverns of this wonderful throbbing building, there is a final frosted glass door that seems to be glowing. It is glowing. It is glowing gold.

I watch the receptionist ooze all the way back to that gold door until she is just a perfect silhouette of a woman, framed in frosted glass that's been lit gold by some incandescent bulb beyond it. She does not look back at me as she opens the door and is bathed and then subsumed by gold. And then the door shuts.

I keep walking until I am close enough I can read the words on the door, each writ carefully in an olde worlde serif.

"Herein, a Registered Business offering Taxation Relief, Investment Support and the Rectifying of Undeclared Incomes."

I turn and, way out in the distance, the entrance to the hallway is just a pinhole of light I have to run for, each step a battle against massive air conditioning currents that are dragging me back and even after I escape the darkness of the hallway, somehow, it, the darkness, follows me out onto the street, where it should be dusky purple summer night but it's not. Clouds have come from nowhere to blot the sunset in the west and the stars in the east. This happens sometimes, night rain, in summer, in Aspenroot. The heat from the city rises up to hit cool air coming over the mountains.

I call a car and squint into blackness while I wait.

I have only one place left to go.

Kristy Lee McIllvinney does not answer the door to her apartment. But I try the knob and find it unlocked, like it was left open just for me. So I go in and her closet is empty and in the bathroom her toothbrush is gone and back in the bedroom I stand for a long time until I notice one other thing. Her great-grandpa's antique shotgun is missing.

And I think, where is Kristy Lee? And did Chekhov's gun maybe have bullets in it after all? And if so, why did she sleep with a loaded shotgun above her bed? And I think the answer to this last question is, "Joe Mead."

Chapter 18
Interrogation

There's a surplus of things in my house that look like they could be Dashain. Like for instance a space heater on the floor. Or a black pair of house slippers, which I don't know why I own because I almost never remember to take my sneakers off when I walk into my house. As I walk around, I constantly think I see him, Dashain, but it's never him because he is mostly always on my bed. He's like my idol, he does nothing so well.

When I get back from Kristy Lee's apartment, I start trying to figure out what happened to Joe Mead with a new urgency. Dashain comes and sits on my lap to help me research/stalk this man. His social feeds have been abandoned and he has a super common name, but the Super Slaughter was big news and there has to be a trail somewhere.

The first item I find is a newspaper story which tells me Joe Mead was put on a sabbatical by his security company immediately after the Super Slaughter. This isn't uber surprising, but it does give me the name of his security company.

Putting his name and former employer together I get to another item, where some intrepid reporter spun up a human interest story about the survivors of mass shootings and how it impacted their lives. Some of them actually found renewed purpose, believed they had a responsibility to do good things for mankind, quit their jobs, joined the Peace Corps or whatever. Others didn't and just kind of went on day after day, slowly going back to the same jobs and lives and families and routines they had beforehand.

The reporter didn't find Joe Mead, but she did interview a friend of his named Robin Gotterdam who said Joe had just kind of knocked around for a while, living on couches, being kind of lost.

Robin Gotterdam is a much easier name to Webworld. And I find that a couple years ago, someone named Robin Gotterdam had been arrested by the APD for hijacking cars. Apparently, Robin would hide out in car washes and, when the door closed, start banging on the windows wearing a Halloween mask, which sounds scary as fuck. In fact, seeing a Halloween mask in your car window in a car wash that you're literally locked inside sounds like the most terrifying thing I can imagine. And then Robin would show the driver a baseball bat or whatever and threaten to smash the window and the driver would get out and try to avoid the hot water while Robin got in his car and safely drove off. Robin was apparently an idiot though, because he did two years in jail because he got caught after a driver left his wallet behind and Robin decided to use his, the driver's, credit card to buy groceries. And while I'm reading this absolutely terrifying story on this police blotter-style blog, and my stomach is kinda twisting as I imagine what it'd be like to look outside my window and see a killer clown mask or whatever, I keep thinking to myself that to really make that plan work, there'd have to be two bad guys. Two. Because otherwise the driver might just get out and kick your ass, right?

And then my stomach really does flip, because I scroll down and right after the story about the carwash hijacking, I see another story, this one about $20,000,000 in diamonds and precious metals being stolen off a jet on a runway in Las Vegas, precisely fifteen months ago.

You know what would make me relax about tracking down the jerkoff who stole a briefcase of diamonds and precious metals from me? If I was still unsure exactly how I was going to offload the other 19 briefcases.

And while I am indulging this paranoid supervillain fantasy, there is a knock at my front door.

I open it because I am an idiot and no one is there.

I step outside, also because I am an idiot, and I feel, not see, a movement beside me, a displacement of the darkness, a giant breath in and then a push out, like a shark rushing to meet a seal at the surface, and I must be the seal because very quickly for me there is only doormat and stars.

I wake up, hands behind my back, tied to a folding chair. It's not a very sturdy folding chair. I could tip it over. But it's made of the awful thin aluminum all folding chairs are made of. It might bend, but it'd never break. So if I tipped it over, then I'd still be tied to an aluminum chair, but instead of sitting in it I'd be lying in it on my side on the ground which sounds more painful, not less.

In front of this aluminum chair and therefore me, the person tied to it, there is a green awful folding lightweight aluminum card table. There is a brownie in the middle of it, centered upon a paper towel.

Past the brownie, there is an honest-to-god typewriter, not a computer, not a word processor, a typewriter, and beside the typewriter there is a short stack of blank paper.

Past the typewriter and the stack of blank paper sits the man I saw at the Cash Register building. At least, I assume it is the same man. It is the same mask, the English one with the imperial and the smile. The man is wearing a black hoodie and black gloves. The hood on the hoodie is pulled up so this man is basically just a mask as far as I am concerned.

Around us, there are floor-to-ceiling aluminum rods on which have been hung floor-to-ceiling curtains. The curtains hide the walls. The ceiling is the awful beige one you might find anywhere, in any suburban home, in any hotel room, with a vague texturing carelessly applied beneath the paint, which was also carelessly applied.

My head hurts so much it doesn't hurt, like it's numb. I try to reach my hand up to feel for a knot where the man clonked me, and there's a quick searing pain as a rope digs into my wrists. My wrists aren't numb at all, unfortunately. They're really letting me down.

I try to turn my head to look down behind me, to where my wrists are tied, but I can't get my neck to swivel that far and pretty soon I give up and settle back into the chair, relax into my restraints, and wait.

The mask/man picks a sheet of paper up into his gloved hand and holds it up, turning it so I can see nothing is written on either side. Then he inserts it into his typewriter and turns the carriage and pecks at the keyboard. When he is done, he turns the carriage again to free the paper. It sounds like someone shuffling a deck of cards.

He slides the paper past the brownie, keeps one finger on it while I read:

Why were you at Cash Register?

I check in with myself. Is my heart racing? Is my stomach churning? How do I feel about this?

I look back at the paper and notice the words have started swimming. Letters are all just symbols, and like the frames of a filmstrip, they have to be arranged in the right order by someone who can create a story from them. After a few seconds they, the letters, swim into the intended order again.

Why were you at Cash Register?

Now I become objectively conscious of how nervous I am. "Stalking a girl I'd recently slept with" is a factually accurate and yet totally terrifying answer for whatever it reveals about me. But do I lie to this human who has me at a bit of a disadvantage? I decide to say something which, while true, is not all of the truth and therefore might be considered a lie by some people.

"I..."

Holy crap, I can't hear my own voice! It's just a bubble at the surface of a pond which I am apparently lying at the bottom of.

"I had..."

My voice doesn't seem to cast an echo. Is it being absorbed by the curtains? Am I more concussed than I thought?

The man tilts his mask face and he spins his finger, motioning for me to get on with it. It looks like he, at least, can hear me. And there is something almost supernaturally charismatic about him, in the angle of his chin or the slope of his shoulders or the clarity of his gestures. I want to obey.

"I had an errand downtown and stopped in for coffee. That's it."

I shouldn't have said "that's it." I know this as soon as I say it. It sounds defensive. It tells him there is more to my story. Two extra words turned my half-truth into a whole-

144

lie.

The masked man's spinning finger stops spinning and starts wagging back and forth - *no no no*.

He taps the paper again.

Why was I at the Cash Register building? I wonder if he'd understand that even I don't really know the answer to this.

"I know this girl who works there."

The man drums his fingertips on the table. He's thinking.

He rolls a new sheet of paper into the typewriter. Again the cards shuffle, again the frame skips, again the keys clack. He is trying to bring order to a different story, I realize. A story in which I am a side character, one who may be a red herring.

He lays the second sheet of paper on top of the first.

Do you know Kristy Lee?

"No," I hear my voice say from the bottom of the pond where I am clearly drowning.

He leans back in his chair and makes a show of first spreading and then folding his arms. He knows I am lying.

I try to reel it back. "I mean, I have a friend who knows her. I don't know her."

He leans forward and spins up a fresh sheet. He types a bit and hits the carriage return for a new paragraph. The clacking is getting louder. Is he hitting the keys harder or am I getting either less or more conscious? Eventually he spins the wheels and flutters this third sheet down on top of the second sheet.

Too late.

Stay away from the Cash Register.

The Super Slaughter was just the beginning.

The man leans in towards me. Slowly, he reaches down with one glove and lifts the brownie, the one that has been sitting on the middle of the cheap card table this whole time, up to my lips and, a slave, I open wide so he can feed me.

Pond water churns around my head. Curtains collapse around my face. The mask blooms into an orchid and then winks into a dying star.

When I wake up, the man has taken me back home. It is also possible I never left home, that he had knocked me out and taken me in the house and used curtains to hide my own walls from me. But either way, I am home now. I know this because I am lying on my back on my family room floor by my fireplace and Dashain is napping, deadweight on my chest.

This is very much where anyone not me would call the police. But I am not not-me. In fact, I am a pretty questionable person these days.

I make myself drink some coffee, but my headache is not a caffeine headache, it is a headache born of being clonked on the head and then fed an extremely toxic version of something that didn't erase my memory, but certainly scrambled it. I remember the English mask that anarchists wear. I remember being warned that I should stay away from the Cash Register building. I remember Kristy Lee is missing and this man, the man in the mask, knows her, too.

It crosses my mind, for the first time ever, that maybe I should at least consider having a WAR cam or even the new Webworld WAR 2 cam installed in my doorbell.

Chapter 19
Inertia

It smells like sour milk but also like night. Sour night.

I love how quiet it always is when I park my truck at Moo Cow early, early Sunday morning. My delivery truck is filled with empties. People don't do a good job rinsing the used milk containers but on a summer night, I can drive with the windows down and it's OK. I have come to associate this sour scent with safety.

I rectify my remaining products against the order sheets and I take all the empty bottles people have returned and I carry them in several trips back into the warehouse where they have this assembly line where first a special sprayer on a nozzle washes them, and then another nozzle sprays some sort of germ killing thing in them, and then the conveyor belt steps even another step farther where a third nozzle rinses them, and then they get pushed through this giant blower that blows up into their waiting mouths and the most amazing thing is that the motor of this device runs completely silently. The conveyor belt is barely noticeable to the people who work it and the people who see it. We all only know it's running because we can see and hear the impact of the various sprays and blows upon the bottles.

It only takes sixty seconds or so and then each bottle is good to go, to be refilled with milk and put back out into the world. I think the conveyer runs all the time, even when the bottles aren't there. It'd take too much energy to power it back up, so they just let it go all day and all night long.

There are no windows back there, so when I sidle through the doors into the little room where the apparently-not-teenage girl works, the first inkling of dawn light blurring on her window feels like equator-level solar energy to me.

I reach one hand up to shield my eyes and she looks at me, amused.

"Well, hello," she says.

She is back in her Moo Cow uniform, which is not an actual uniform or even anything resembling professional clothing. She's wearing sweatpants on her legs and a flannel shirt and her hair is pulled into a ponytail and she's not wearing any makeup at all, but she doesn't seem to need it, because her skin is perfect, as fresh, white and soft as hotel room pillows. I look for bleary sleep rings under her eyes and see nothing except a tiny crinkle, as if she is trying very hard not to laugh at me.

"You ever get tired?"

She shakes her head no.

"Working two jobs?"

She shrugs, "It's all the same job and it's called making a living."

"You know, I do some trading downtown," I am not sure what most people mean by trading, although in my case it has something to do with selling diamonds for subjective amounts of cash, "and I have a girl I eat lunch with sometimes," I am really struggling, and I am struggling with struggling because I want to ask her about Kristy Lee but my very male brain also doesn't want to tell this girl about Kristy Lee because ever since I saw that tattoo or pen doodle ringing her perfect thigh I have been trying to suppress the knowledge that my body finds her body very hot, "but she hasn't been around and I was wondering, do you know the people in the Cash Register building?"

She, the receptionist, is really enjoying my doofusness, I can tell. "Some by face. Some by name. All by their accounts and records."

"Really?"

"It's just amazing how much us lowly workers know, shuffling papers, mailing checks. I do think I know more about more than most people alive."

"Her name is Kristy Lee McIllvinney."

"Tell me, what does this Kristy Lee McIllvinney look like?"

"Blonde. Mid-thirties maybe. She works at Cash Register."

"The actual Cash Register? Most of the Cash Register

150

building is subletted to various enterprises."

"Yeah, I guess I saw. What kind of enterprises?"

"Oh, all the fun ones. Marketing agencies. Virtual reality. Video gaming. Content creators. App developers. Film producers. Streaming platforms. All just salesmen who assign value to pixels and dreams."

"SuperMeme?"

"What's left of them. Only a couple people work there these days."

"Ever see a man visit SuperMeme named... *Joe Mead*?"

She sucks in her breath, interested suddenly, examining me with the enraptured curiosity of a second-grade scientist watching rats run a maze. "Joe Mead?" she teases, holding the name out there like a bit of cheese. "Why, I thought this conversation was about Kristy Lee McIllvinney?"

"It was. It is. Have you seen her?"

"Not for a couple days, I guess. I suppose I may have missed her, though. My job keeps me very busy."

"And what job is that?"

"Oh, I'm just a receptionist."

"You like that? Being a receptionist?"

"Very much."

And I start thinking I have had the wrong answer to everything all along. Maybe the answer was never Joe Mead. Maybe the answer has always been a different name, the name of the little person, the assistant who died especially, died for what seemed like no reason at all.

Rowan McGregor.

I have to shake my head to clear my mind and get back on track, because the real reason I started talking to this specific girl - at least the real reason I think I started talking to this specific girl - is that I am worried about her. In fact, I have been worrying about her quite a bit for the past couple of days. What if the guy who knocked me out re-enacted the Super Slaughter at the Cash Register building? What if Christopher Gouldberg didn't act alone? What if this girl, the one in front of me, is in danger?

"You know," I say, "I've heard there's copycats out there. Who think the Super Slaughter, the one at SuperMeme, that it was just the beginning. Maybe you ought to let that job go? Focus on this Moo Cow thing?"

And the girl rolls her eyes at me and then very slowly and considerately puts her middle finger right in front of my face.

"OK," I say, stepping backwards. "You be careful, then."

My bike is chained up to the stair rail on the side of Moo Cow. It's pretty well lit back there, and the sun is pretty much up anyway, and the big roller doors are open and I can hear work crews loading and cleaning, bringing in milk and cream for whoever makes Sunday night deliveries. But now there is, standing next to it, my bike, a shadow. A dark shadow of a man dressed in clothes the color that black, navy and charcoal clothes all become after a few trips through the washing machine.

The man isn't looking at me, but I stop thirty feet away

and watch as he pulls a cigarette and a cigarette lighter out of his pocket and as he sparks up I can see the scars twisting across half his face.

He puts his lighter back in his pocket, and, cigarette dangling from the soft side of his mouth, ambles off east, towards the risen sun.

Gulp.

I am not 100% sure I feel safe going home and in fact am not 100% sure I feel safe anywhere right now, but Dashain is at home and I think he'll act as a very sleepy early warning system should anyone with a half-face, single foot or white mask attempt to break into the house. So home is where I bike alongside early morning traffic, happy families going to church and so forth. Every so often, I veer off the main road and park my bike behind a fir tree and wait for a minute to make sure nobody is following me. And about the third time I do this I realize that while being followed would be sort of terrifying, it is even more terrifying not to be followed because it means they, whoever *they* are, already know where I live.

I walk my bike up onto my front porch with my head on a swivel, looking into the bushes, looking back over my shoulder. I am scared to unlock the door, because that would require an inordinate amount of time looking down at the doorknob, inserting my key and so forth. So I lay my bike down on the grass, twirl around and sit out there on my front step for a while, my face inches from my phone.

Rowan McGregor's ProPro is still active. I wonder at

what point it will come down, who'll let whoever controls this corner of Webworld know she is dead and who will be trusted to make the decision what to do with her ProPro page.

Meanwhile the ad alongside Rowan's ProPro asks me if I want to see jobs that match my skills. I almost tap this ad, just to find out exactly what skills this professional social platform thinks I have.

Rowan's bio says she was an assistant in SuperMeme/Aspenroot's accounts payable department. The job description, which she must have written herself, says, "I make sure every payment is penny accurate and as prompt as practical." Her ProPro picture could not be more peppy. Tight curls rimming her round face. Round eyes and no chin. The hint of a floral pattern on her collar.

Rowan's old social accounts are sometimes private and sometimes not, but a Webworld image search for her utterly unique name turns up many more happy pictures. Plenty of check-ins at this restaurant and that bar.

Now my phone serves me an ad encouraging me to search restaurants for open reservations tonight.

My thumb scrolls past the ad and stops on one Rowan-pic, kinda blurry. In it she has redeye, and she is clearly holding the phone out, trying to frame a selfie of herself and someone she's with. This someone has a round head. This someone has a crewcut, blond hair tight over a fleshy skull. This someone is trying to get out of the frame. He is turning to his left, the frame's right. And his right shoulder is coming up a bit and his right ear is dipping down, like his shoulder might somehow hide his cheek. His right nostril is flaring in surprise.

I look at this half of a man's face for a long time.

Joe Mead, is that you?

I can't tell. But I can read the caption beneath the photo.

"After work drinks at Confluence!!! First time here!"

Confluence. I have heard of this bar before. Kristy Lee said it was Joe Mead's favorite watering hole.

Whir, click, the scenes start to fall into place.

Chapter 20
The Story of Jason ZZ

"Not so many years ago there was a car only came out at night. The skin was a matte black gritty and flat as southeast Kansas two-lane blacktop. The spoiler was a glossy black, waxed so it reflected all of Aspenroot back up to the moon, frien'. And the windows been tinted so dark you could probably host your New Year's Eve do-up in there and nobody'd see the confetti or the flashing lights.

"Behind this car's wheel only ever sat Jason ZZ, late of the Bronx's fearsome ZZ Tribe. He'd cut his teeth running corners for Macc ZZ and then killing fools for Bronx's king and thug-for-life, Mark tha First ZZ. Eventually, Jason rolled west to find larger land to colonize, dead set on setting up ZZ Tribe Aspenroot just as big and scary as ZZ Tribe Bronx ever been. He kept his hair real short, because people should be able to make his eyes. He wore a white leather jacket two sizes too big, because he wanted everyone could see him coming. He had a Z inked on his right hand

and a Z inked on his left, because it could be no other way.

"Sometimes people got out of line because sometimes people got dumb. Jason handled infraction one just like Mark tha First ZZ had done. Up close, eye to eye, no known enforcers in tow. He believed the thing Mark tha First ZZ'd taught him: people needed to fear the man, not just the name, though the name be ZZ.

"Numero uno on his list tonight: dude name of Robin. He was a liquor store roller, a dime bag dealer, an occasional able body in the crew of a smarter hombre. But word had got back to Jason ZZ. Robin had himself a partner and they'd stumbled onto something that'd been making them (and the guy ran the chop shop on Van Nickington) something approaching wealthy men.

"Now frien', the way Jason ZZ saw it, he didn't need a cut of every damn thing that happened in his hood. Mark tha First ZZ never demanded tribute, and he still kept mad and total respect. But if a crew had an ongoing thing – carjacking or otherwise – that very much needed to be ZZ Tribe Aspenroot's business. But had Robin and his phantom shotcaller looped Jason ZZ in? No, they mos' def had not.

"The all-black ride rolled south. The engine growled when the traffic moved, purred when it didn't. Jason ZZ kept one hand on the wheel, not in much of a hurry. He was heading towards the block where street wisdom said Robin liked to do his social drinking. He figured this soon post-jack, the man would be keeping it real cheap, staying tight to his block, and spinning stories about how he definitely had nothing going on.

"Jason ZZ parked the car at a meter and fed it with silver, because using his credit card would place him square on a block where shit might be about to get real. He buttoned his white leather so it helped conceal the bump where his piece got stuck down the front of his pants. And then he ambled westward, sticking his head in dive after dive, asking the heinas he saw if they'd recently run into a cat name of Robin, Robin Gotterdam.

"They finally bumped in this very dark room where you and me sit, frien', this dark room on Gilbert Road with a sign out front, Confluence. When Jason ZZ walked in, he saw that up in front the bar was gettin' average folks good and liquored so they could dance to the songs sung by a pretty white woman in a pretty white dress, backed by one old man slappin' skins and another old man strappin' on a Tele with flames 'cross the top. This trio played to a crowd three-dozen strong: a bride to be, her spinning courtesans, a happy-go-lucky Asian guy and a drunk Mexican man spinning a Samoan lover who outweighed him double.

"A brave and fall-down drunk old man abandoned the safety of the rail and waddled out on the dance floor, wearing navy jog pants and a turquoise Polo shirt. He shrugged his shoulders until he found the rhythm and then he began to shake, lifting one leg and then the other. And he did not dance with the bride and he seemed to care only for himself and the melody and so the people rimming the dance floor soon cared only for him and they smiled, as if they all had been born purely to cheer for him as he showed them how to love their lives, their bodies and the music they shared.

"Jason ZZ had no time for that noise! He pushed his way through the crowd to where Robin was shooting pool with me. That's right, my frien' and drink procurer. Was me the whole time, listenin' good, swear. He, Robin just chilling in his red flannel and jeans. Robin's hair was cropped tight and his whiskers had been growing a week and a day. His sleeves were rolled up to reveal a self-inflicted tat on his right forearm that read, man, who could tell? Jason ZZ got hisself a drink from the heina at the counter and then sat making eyes at Robin till Robin finally snapped to. The man's eyes got all big and scared, and his fingers went white around that pool cue. He sniffed, steadied himself and said a bit too loud across the room, 'Jason ZZ, what is up?'

"Jason ZZ made a silly face, a comedy-movie vogue, and shifted his shoulders left and right in a slow-mo dance hall jive. This was his night, this was his hood, no reason he couldn't enjoy himself. More important, Jason ZZ wanted to show motherfuckin' Robin that, yep, this was how a ZZ had fun.

"He slid off his stool and came sashaying his sweet way across the floor. 'Thought that was you. How you feeling?'

"'I'm good,' Robin said. But he didn't look good. His fingers were playing slip and slide with the pool cue. 'You?'

"'Aw baby,' Jason ZZ said. He extended his fist. 'If I

had your hand.'

"Robin took a wet palm off the pool cue and knuckle tapped the Z of Jason ZZ's fist.

"Jason ZZ looked at the guy'd been shooting with Robin - me, sweet and dirty all at once. Jason ZZ didn't give two shits either way, goes, 'My friend, whyn't you skate a way aways?'

"Me, I mumbled something about being mid-rack, and Robin's face went from up tight to Imma-gonna-puke like it be sixty seconds till four a.m.. He turned and stuttered at me, 'No, no. You gotta go.'

"I took another look at Jason ZZ, who was relaxed, a little smile hanging out on his face as he enjoyed this tense little moment in time. I went, 'Whatever,' and didn't make eye contact with absolutely anybody as I shuffled towards the bar. But I didn't go so far I couldn't hear what was said up in there. So my story stays genuine, swear.

"'Been a bit,' Robin said to Jason ZZ.

"'True, true. You used to call. We used to ball. Now what do you do?'

"'Me? Nothing. I ain't been working.'

"'Gosh-golly that sounds rough.'

"'You got a job for me?' Robin trying to make his voice sound eager.

"Jason ZZ cocked his head and made bug eyes at Robin till the man couldn't take no more, turned, and began re-racking the pool balls. Jason ZZ kept quiet because that's what predators do when their prey making a fool of itself.

'"Listen..."

'"Cain't when you're facing t'other way."

Robin turned, stood tall, trying to be brave. He and Jason ZZ were almost the same size, almost the same height. But only one'd carved a Z on a man's face at a club because he asked for his own heina back. (Street had it the entire club had borne witness, yet the bouncers swore they hadn't heard a thing.)

'"Listen, Jason ZZ, I been working a little, you're right. But it ain't nothing regular or I would've kept you in the know. You know I'm like that."

'"What little?"

"Robin swallowed. 'Jacked a car?'

'"One car?"

'"Couple."

'"Couple?"

'"We were gonna say..."

'"Ah!' Jason ZZ flattened his palms and raised the roof. 'We. Now that is an interesting pronoun. Who is, I gotta know, we?'

'"Just a guy guy."

'"Name him."

'"He..."

'"Name this boy, ain't think to come to talk to me."

'"His name's..."

'"'Cause if the next word out're yer mouth isn't Jesus Christ? Mmm!'

"'It wasn't…'

"'What?'

"'It wasn't Jesus Christ, Jason ZZ. I…'

"'You don't say?'

"'No, I…'

""'Cause I figured Robin steppin' out on his own, it better be with a crew led by the lord of mankind and all the animals. Big ol' beard. Like his robes all flappin' out behind him.' Jason ZZ sashayed his hands behind him. 'Runnin' around like, "Follow me 'cause I'm the Jesus!"'

"'Joe.'

"'Joe?'

"'No, swear. Joe Mead.'

"'Hm.' Jason ZZ tapped his chin. 'You know, I think I did hear tell of that Jesus impersonator. Liquor store knockovers, muscleman from time to time for this set 'n that. Tough guy. So you like him better'n you like me?'

"'No, Jason ZZ. Not like that. Just a thing we did.'

"But Jason ZZ was having much fun, and could not be bothered to hear Robin's plea. 'I'm so sexy and shit. He must be tough, you like him so much. Mad skills and so forth.'

"'It was his idea. He said…'

"'Mm hm? Go on.'

"'He said he didn't need to cut you in, that you'd be cool, made it sound like he had some sort of connection.' Robin connected dots, concocted what passed for a game plan. The words rushed out of him. 'So Jason ZZ, see, I thought his connection was to you. I thought he'd checked with you. So I figured we were already cool.'

"'I love homeboys lyin' to me. Love 'em so much!' Robin tried to interrupt and Jason ZZ shushed him still. 'Hush, boy. We're past that. Plan is, I'll talk to your boy, Joe Mead. Sounds like me and him need to have what they call a meeting of the minds. But you have a separate expectation, and it rhymes with "five grand in twenty-four hours." Then, we'll be a'ight again.'

"'I…'

"'You drop the money with any of my fourteen corners. They'll get at me.'

"Jason ZZ stepped forward and pursed his lips while he surveyed the pool table. 'You wanna shoot a rack with me? No? You don't look like you do. 'Nother time then, bro. 'Nother time.'

"Frien', next time Jason ZZ got seen, you know where it was? *Do you know?* He'd got his naked self superglued fifteen feet high on a wall downtown and then someone'd cut him open 'cross his belly. Jason ZZ bled to death with his stomach and his liver and shit sloppin' down over his thighs, down on them same sidewalks he once aimed to rule.

"So no, don't care how bad you are, skinny white boy. Don't care how much you want to know. I don't care! No matter what you do, don't go pushin' for no stories about Joe Mead. Because you know who that connection them boys discussed must have been? Who that single man was,

163

bold enough to do that to a ZZ tribe? You know what man left his signature on that sidewalk, a shiny top hat placed like a bucket to fill up with Jason ZZ's own blood?"

I shook my head.

And the drunk man leaned close and whispered fierce, "Chatterhat."

Chapter 21
Prevarications

I managed to stay pretty sober at Confluence. It'd seemed like a dive at first, no big deal. But by halfway through the drunk guy's awesome story, I was in mortal fear of essentially everyone in there.

So the next day I wait for it to be bright and utter sunlight and then leave my house to knock on the door of Simon and Mindy, my neighbors. But two things occur to me.

First, it is unlikely they will answer, since it is the middle of a Monday and that is clearly when most people are off doing what they have to to make money so they can afford a house with a front door.

Second, they almost certainly have a WAR camera

which would record me knocking on their door, which would lead them to naturally wonder why I'd come over, which would ruin my illusion of spontaneity.

So I do a U-turn back inside my house and, starting at four in the afternoon, I watch their driveway from my front window, and when I see Simon pull up in his brown-wrapper sedan, I pop out my front door, basketball in hand, and start dribbling my way up the sidewalk. We wave at each other. He's in his garage, pulling his briefcase out of the backseat of the sedan, and I stop my dribble as if I just thought of something, which is, of course, something I have actually been rehearsing pretty much all day.

"Simon," I say.

"Bob, how you doing?"

I am surprised that I am not even surprised that Simon knows my name now. I have successfully moved from one identity to the next. From Rob, aimless if affable young man from a moderately wealthy family taking a gap year out of college, to Bob, kind of quiet but nice neighbor who works from home and must be pretty successful at some nebulous something.

"Good, I'm good."

"You here about the neighborhood watch?"

"The what?"

"The watch the ladies are setting up. To help watch for whatever it is that's been taking the cats?"

"Oh," I say. "Makes sense, but hey..."

This lie I have concocted is not even close to the truth.

My first idea had been to say a friend who was in some trouble mentioned Chatterhat to me. But that lie would be uber easy for Simon to check and even if he didn't, he might decide to take an interest in my imaginary friend's nonexistent case. So instead, I go for the whopper.

"I was out with some friends the other night. And there's this new drinking game called Chatterhat."

Simon very slowly closes his car door and turns full on to face me. The neighbor guy I knew is trying to stay in control, but justice guy, alpha guy, that guy is clearly swimming to the surface and this other identity of Simon is looking at me from behind my suburban neighbor's suddenly small eyes.

I plow forward.

"And I asked about it and people were saying it's based on some true crime case. I was wondering if you ever heard of it? Like, is there really a Chatterhat?"

He deliberates and then non-answers. "There is a drinking game called Chatterhat?"

"You have to hide a penny under beer coasters."

"There," he says, "is no 'true crime case' behind Chatterhat. It's a generic term for a money launderer. You know what a money launderer is?"

"Kind of?"

"It's someone who takes the money a white collar criminal or a drug dealer just got and filters it through fake businesses so the bad guy can use it to buy a car or a house or whatever."

"Like a pawn shop for stolen goods?"

"Not really. A step beyond that. Like, the accountant you need after you sell your stolen goods. You have to find ways to report income that can't be tracked."

"So Chatterhat is a money launderer?"

"There is no Chatterhat."

"No?"

"Got it?"

"Yeah, sure."

"Bob, it's a generic term. Like, 'I got to find a Chatterhat.' There is no Chatterhat."

This doesn't square at all with what Robin's pool partner told me. But what can I say?

"Huh," I say.

Simon is regarding me with much interest. More than I am strictly comfortable with. "Bob, what exactly is it that you do for a living?"

"I'm like a consultant of sorts. Tech. IT. Social media. Searching for things."

"I was talking to Dana and Greg the other night."

Oh no.

"Dana said she thought you were an investor."

Oh, OK. I think, because I thought Dana had sold me out, told everybody I was the neighborhood milkman. But this is much better. "Yeah," I say, "I have some investments."

"What kind of investments would those be, Bob?"

Shoot, now I am thinking maybe it would've been

better if she had sold me out. I say something about commodities.

Gold is a commodity. So it's not totally a lie, is it?

Chapter 22
Returns

I do not Webworld Chatterhat. I am terrified to a degree where I think I'm going to throw up. More terrified, even, than I was of the man in the white mask.

What if Simon decides maybe I am more suspicious than he suspected and deserve a little governmental surveillance? Or what if he was lying to me? What if there is a Chatterhat or multiple Chatterhats and they can see what I search, know what names I type into my phone?

Kristy Lee McIllvinney.

Rowan McGregor.

Joe Mead.

I power down, literally, my phone for the first time in years, literally. And as it vibrates its way off, there is another vibration in my home, a rapid but soft flutter of knocks coming from my front door.

But I definitely do not go to my front door. I run upstairs, taking steps two at a time. Dashain is sleeping on my pillow and he only barely opens one eye as I go diving over him to my bedroom window and peer down and wait.

It is pink weekday dusk outside. It is very quiet, until suddenly down the street rumbles a boxy food truck with a sign on it that says, "Crazy Suzy's Fish Stew." Does one of my neighbors have a food truck? They seem to be a popular hobby for rich people. The truck bumps over to the side of the curb and I hear the squeak of an emergency brake being pulled. The engine cuts off, but no one gets out.

Now there's motion directly beneath my window. The person who had been rapping on my door has given up, and I see the top of a familiar blond head as she steps off my porch into the pink-gray evening and hesitates, eyeing the food truck that has rudely arrived.

"Kristy Lee," I stage-whisper out my window.

She whips her head around.

"Up here."

She looks up, but to her, looking from evening light into indoor dark, I must just be a shadow. "Bob?"

"Hold on," I stage-whisper again.

I scramble downstairs and, as I go, I am smoothing my hair and making sure my fly is up. I open the door and she practically runs through it.

"Sorry," I say, letting her push past me. "I think I think I am being watched."

She is carrying a duffel bag and a locking long gray case. I am sure that inside it, that locking long gray case, is a loaded and operational shotgun.

"You're being watched, too?"

I am not sure what or how much to tell her. But she doesn't let me say anything anyway. She sets down her bag and her case and looks behind her at the solidly locked door. She jiggles the lock a few times and then asks me if my back door is locked, too.

"Yeah, sure."

"Sure?"

"Kristy Lee, where have you been?"

"What do you mean?"

"I've been trying to get hold of you."

She nods in a way that feels a little dismissive. "Oh yeah. True. Well, for the first couple days you were texting me, I was messing with you. I was just busy. But I was going to text you back, I promise."

"It's fine. But?"

"Friday, I was alone in the restroom on my floor at Cash Register, washing my hands. All alone. And the door flies open! And suddenly there's this man in there with me, blocking the door. And he was wearing a mask. Like one of those Guy Hawks masks."

"You mean from Anonymous? I think it's named…"

"No, I think it was from a movie."

"Well, I think the movie was from a comic."

"Oh my god, it doesn't make a difference, Bob."

"OK."

"So I started to scream because, like, was he going to attack me? But he held up one hand, one black glove, and it was like I can't even explain it. Like he'd hypnotized me with that one wave. Next thing I know I am standing there, very straight, water dripping off my hands, facing him. And then he bowed."

"Bowed?"

"Like this." And Kristy Lee binds her left forearm behind her back and lifts her right hand in the air and then bows from the waist, all the way down, down until her hide-me-not nose is pointing at the floor and damn near level with her hips.

She straightens back up and now I'm the one hypnotized and she takes off her jacket and hands it to me. Underneath she's wearing just jeans and a tank top.

My house is getting pretty dark now but that feels right, so I leave the lights off and we move through the shadows into the main room on my first floor, the one with the fireplace in the wall and the tennis ball marks on the ceiling. I hope Kristy Lee doesn't look up. And I realize, she is the first human I have ever been alone in my home with. Unless you count (maybe) the guy in the mask, who I am still not sure if he was in my home or some other undefined space.

Kristy Lee goes to sit cross-legged on the floor by the fireplace and I reach out, take her hand to steady her as she goes down. And then I go without asking into my kitchen and I get her some wine from a bottle I still have left over from my party.

When I hand it down to her, she smiles. "So gallant."

"Me?"

"Yeah, sure. But the man was who I was thinking. He bowed so deeply, it was so gallant. And I wasn't scared. He was like a magician and I only existed for him, to be a character in his act. He waved his hand in the air and, poof, there was a note in it. And he placed the note on the sink and with one finger he pushed it my way. And then he waved goodbye and he backed up, away from me, through the door. And he was gone. Bob, I can't explain it. I didn't want him to go. I felt sad. I wanted to chase him, beg him to let me follow. But I didn't. I let him go. And I lifted the note off the sink and it read, 'Stay away from the Cash Register building. You may be in danger. The Super Slaughter was just the beginning.'"

I want to tell her he was here too, at my home, maybe in my home. But if she asks why he might warn me to stay away from the Cash Register building, that means I have to admit I have been in the Cash Register building. (I think.) So I just mumble exactly what she said, like I am thinking it over, "The Super Slaughter was just the beginning."

"It was typed. The note. Like, with a typewriter."

I lower myself down onto the floor to sit across from her.

"Bob, after the Super Slaughter, two days later, the day after Christmas, I went back to the office to get my things, and I expected it to be this really lonely, emotional experience. Like, I brought tissues and stuff. But instead when I opened the doors there were people *everywhere*, like

174

they'd been waiting the whole time, hiding in our closets and our desk drawers, and suddenly these people all just popped out like ants and went to work. And they didn't look like advertising people, Bob. They wore gray suits and ugly glasses and they all sat down at our computers and were opening files and closing them and opening files and closing them. And I couldn't handle it. I just turned around and left. And then when I came back the next day to try again to get my stuff, now there were only two people, these two drab new people, and they said they were business development people who were there to help rebuild the office, like, talk to clients and stuff. They said they had been hired by New York. But here's the thing." She reached across my lap to take my hand. "I think they were two of the same people I saw the day before. Like, they wore better clothes, but they were so boring. They said the corporate honchos had hired them to assure the Aspenroot clients that SuperMeme was there for them and they would rebuild the office or, if the clients weren't into that, they could choose to work with SuperMeme's coastal teams, who really were the Webworld experts after all. But these two new people, I never saw them do anything. Ever. They told me their names were Adam and Eve. I was like, nope. I worked from home for two months and didn't do anything, not for a single day. I just sat in my apartment and watched TV and I got paid anyway. Every week. And finally I got my new job at Cash Register and quit. When I heard SuperMeme moved into the Cash Register building a while ago, I even poked my head in. They're on the fourteenth floor. But it was just two people, not Adam and Eve. It was two kids wearing t-shirts. One was watching videos on OurScreen and the other was playing video games. They asked me if they could help me. I was just like, 'Wrong floor.' And they just turned away, went back to staring at their screens. I guess they believed me? I don't know. It's so easy to get mixed up on floors in Cash Register. They're all identical."

"Except that mezzanine one."

"Which one?"

"That first one. Up the escalator."

My voice is trailing off because I realize I should have kept my mouth shut. But maybe it's no big deal because don't most Aspenroot locals walk through Cash Register (the building) at some point in their lives? Like, even to get coffee in the atrium? But then how would I have been on the mezzanine? I am staring down at my drink trying to figure out some story to tell. But Kristy Lee seems to not be worried about this at all, because she says, "I'm not sure what floor you mean. There aren't any offices on the floor by the elevators."

I am not going to argue with her, because - again - I am afraid she's going to ask me what I was doing at Cash Register, when I was there, and why I was exploring the mezzanine.

But I am saved by a knock at the door. It's pretty loud. Me and Kristy Lee look at each other, like, who could this be, and she even whispers, "Who could it be?"

I am grateful the knock distracted her, but also terrified by the multitude of unsavory humans and food truck employees who could be waiting at my front door. So I crawl to my first floor bathroom window to peek out, and now the sun's absolutely down and my porch light has automatically popped on and inside its yellow glow, I see not a half-faced man but two women with faces: Next Door Mindy and It's Fur Josie. They are wearing matching t-shirts, which are red, but I can't read them until I slip out of the bathroom and try, as nonchalantly as possible, to answer the door a crack, not actually opening the screen door.

"Bob," Mindy says, "we are starting a neighborhood watch program to look out for the neighborhood's cats."

"I think I heard about this."

They must have had them specially printed, the t-shirts. They say, in black block letters "Streets & Porches Is Everybody's Safety."

"Clever shirt," I say, but they don't hear me that well or don't care about my opinion and they launch into their spiel. They have a survey they want me to take and I agree, sure, why not?

Josie looks down at the tablet in her hand and taps in my name and then scrolls down to question one, "Would you be in favor of a special referendum allowing a tax up to but not inclusive of 0.05% of a property's valuation to be spent upgrading everybody's WAR to the new Webworld-approved WAR II, which is HD and actually automatically syncs everything to Webworld Data Drawers so we can all have equal access to the video in the event of an, um, event?"

Behind me from someplace far down the hall, I hear Kristy Lee loud-whisper, "Who is it?" I wave my hand behind my butt, which I hope is universal code for go away.

"Um, I'm not sure I have WAR in my house."

"So we'll put you down for yes! You're going to love having one," Josie says. "I do." She, Josie, winks.

Mindy nods. "Simon says they've been a big help. The police can monitor them all the time for porch pirates."

"They can do that?"

"Well, the HOA has to approve it. Do you get the Webworld Calendar invites for our quarterly GridVid chats?"

"Maybe?"

Now Kristy Lee is whispering again, and to me it seems very loud. Almost deafening. "Do you need me to get my gun?"

I wave my hand harder, hard enough that Josie notices.

"You, uh, you ok Bob?"

"Yeah, I just..."

"You have company?"

"No," I say and immediately wonder why. Because it's not like that'd be weird, me having company.

Josie is like, "You look a little disheveled, Bob. Do you have a girlfriend in there?"

"Yeah, maybe." I finger my wrinkled shirt and tangled

hair and in my jeans and no shoes, I got to admit, I do look like I just got up from some bed where I was either napping or otherwise occupied.

"Anyway, for the HOA you're supposed to fill out a proxy if you aren't chatting," Mindy tsk tsk tsks me, but I can tell at this point she is not really mad, more like flirt-teasing when she says, "It's people like you who keep us from having a quorum so we can vote on the sidewalk improvement initiative, the mandatory 10-minute adult swim addendum, the pre-Memorial Day tulip ban..."

Josie says we need to speed it up because there are a lot of other neighbors they need to talk to, no offense, and she just has a few more questions, the next of which we kind of already covered, which is, "Would you be in favor of upgrading the proper governmental authority's ability to access our WAR cam footage from part-time WAR to full-time WW2?"

"I, um..."

"We can put you down for yes. The HOA will have to confirm the vote either way, so it really doesn't mean anything. It's just a formality," Josie says.

"And he already promised he'll be at the next meeting," Mindy reminds her.

"So third question, Bob. 'Do you currently or have you recently owned a cat?'"

I know the answer to this one. "Yes."

"Cute!" Josie marks down yes, I assume. She taps something on her tablet. "What's his or her name?"

"It's a him."

She is not really listening, though, she is scrolling to the final actual formal question on her tablet, which is, "We are thinking of setting up some regular neighborhood patrols to keep an eye out for the goat monster." Behind her, Mindy does air quotes around 'goat monster' and I smile but Josie doesn't notice, because she is still reading, "So the question is, 'Would you be available to walk the neighborhood on a regular basis, either with a partner or alone, to help keep Winegrove's streets and sidewalks safe for everyone?' So? How about it? Are you in?"

I hedge and Mindy tries to sell it with a smile, "SPIES are watching, Bob!"

"Do I get a shirt?"

Josie 100% takes this as a yes. "Yay, awesome. So that concludes our survey. We'll be releasing the results on the Winegrove page on Hoodlife."

"Hoodlife?" I have actually heard of Hoodlife, but...

"It's a social site for neighborhoods. You should join!"

"Yeah, sounds fun."

"Sure it does," Mindy goes to punch my shoulder playfully, but she can't because my screen door is still technically closed so she just kinda pumps her fist awkwardly in the air. "Single guy, hanging out with the Wives of Winegrove. You just go back to whatever you were doing in there, Bob."

The two ladies walk back into the night, armed with nothing but a tablet and two red shirts and I push my door safely shut and lock it and turn around.

My main room seems vacant, but then Kristy pops up from behind the couch and levels her shotgun at me. I make a barking noise and scramble backwards into my hallway and on the hardwood my feet slip and I end up falling onto my butt.

"Do I fire it yet?" she asks me.

"Do you fire what?" I say. I am not even trying to stand up. I'm just looking up at her, panting.

"Chekhov's gun. You said if you see Chekhov's gun in the first act, you better fire it in the third act."

"I'm not sure this is that type of story." I try to explain the goat monster thing.

"You have a monster that creeps into your neighborhood at night and eats pets and I'm supposed to put my shotgun away?"

"It's probably a coyote."

"Did anyone call animal control?"

This is a great question I have not considered.

Kristy Lee lays the shotgun across the couch and sits on the floor, leans back against the cushions and I crawl over to lean next to her.

"I think we're going to get, like, a neighborhood watch program going."

"Private security when what you need is some actual cops."

"Speaking of private security."

"Was I?"

"Well, remember a while ago you said Joe Mead, he was mostly concerned about this one person dying."

"Rowan McGregor."

"Yes, Rowan McGregor."

"She was like, in accounting or something."

"But did she know him, you think? Joe Mead?"

"I don't know. I mean, we all saw him. He was at the front desk. Every day. But Rowan was happy, she seemed happy. They might've hung out."

"Might have."

"You know Bob, I was never happy like she was. I thought I was going to take on the world, break through that glass ceiling. And I was proud when I did it. Proud, walking through that place, SuperMeme/Aspenroot, knowing I was one to watch, that powerful people were hearing good things about me. But I broke through the glass ceiling and found out *there's a prison on the other side.* People are awful to you. Everybody always negotiating and interrupting and stabbing you in the back. SuperMeme was fucking built on bullshit and bluster. It was bankrupt from the beginning. Clients won't pay what an idea is worth. They'll pay for hours and materials. Or they'll let you make up performance metrics and then pay you for hitting those. But selling ideas? It's like selling air. But you know what?"

"What?"

"Cash Register's basically exactly the same. Different industry, but the same bullshit. We invent nonexistent style influencers and film them on a cyclorama in India. Then we give our content away and pay robots to gin up the stats on our websites. Bob, we sell clothes that fall apart on purpose so people will have to rebuy them. It's stupid. Capitalism is a prison and I hate it. I don't want to break through the glass ceiling anymore. I want to go back underneath it and be happy again. I was happy before, back when I was the Princess of Aspenroot and a dashing young king looked at me like we were just characters in a play, a play that could only end one way."

Chapter 23
Whispers

That night, there is another knock at my door. Three visitors in one day is absolutely a new record for me. And I would be overjoyed at this lack of invisibility except that my first knocker, Kristy Lee, is currently 100% passed out next to me in bed and I am not especially eager to leave her. Dashain is sleeping on her belly like he owns her. He opens his eyes and looks at me and in his cat-eyes I see a warning. "Dude, get that door or they are going to knock louder and wake up my new pillow."

Dashain is apparently a 100% traitor.

I get out of bed and try to look down out of my bedroom window to see who is on my porch but the angle is wrong. There's no way to tell. It could be a late-period anarchist planning to finish me off. It could be a goat monster inquiring after my cat. It could be Crazy Suzy's Fish Stew wondering if I have the munchies.

I scamper down the stairs in sweatpants and a t-shirt and stare at my front door. There is a screen door on the other side, but I can't recall if it is locked or even has a lock, which means odds are it is open.

I don't want them to knock louder, but I also don't want to open my door and get mugged and/or eaten. So I do the only even kind-of logical thing I can think of.

I tap on the inside of my own front door.

And from the night on the other side, I hear a coo, "Oh Bob the Milkman, is that you?"

I crack open the door and sure enough, there is a silhouette there framed not by white stars and white moons, but by golden things - streetlights and porch lights. It, this silhouette, looks, based solely on an abundance of chest curve, like it belongs to Dana Supperville.

She says to me, "So, Bob."

"Uh, hey," I say.

"We are in the middle of one of my very special parties. Myself and Greg, and Simon and Mindy, and Jacob and Melinda. And we were just thinking how interesting it would be if you joined us."

Dana is not whispering, exactly. But she doesn't need to talk very loudly either, because it is midnight and this is the suburbs and there's basically nothing that would or could make a competing noise. And her quiet voice makes me remember her whisper voice and the nearness of her body when she used it.

So there's a part of me that wants to go and that part of me really, really wants to go. Like, wants to go more than anything. But Kristy Lee is asleep, like, right upstairs. And it'd be really extra weird if she woke up and I was gone.

"I'm not dressed," I say, though I know this sounds more like a question than a statement.

"Bob, for what I have in mind, you are dressed adorably."

"Ok, but I just need to be back in like an hour."

"Milk route?"

"Something like that," I say.

I go inside and leave a note for Kristy Lee on my kitchen counter. It says, "Had to run out for work. Back by 1 a.m. - I am OK." And I underline "I am OK" several times to make sure she realizes I am ok, and I haven't been kidnapped or something, although I realize I am probably overdoing it and she'll think I have been kidnapped and have been forced to write this note to throw her off the scent.

Once outside, Dana threads her fingers into mine and tiptoes up to lean against me and whisper in my ear, "Stay very, very close to me so we don't set off anybody's cameras. We shouldn't be seen holding hands."

She tugs me down my sidewalk and into the center of the twisty street and we walk down its exact middle together until we reach her house, at which point we take a 90-degree turn and walk up her stairs, past her porch swing and inside.

Her husband and the other four people are all standing around the room and the first one to come skipping up to me is Melinda. She has a single drink clasped in both hands and she keeps it in both hands so that it is physically between us as she leans up toward my ear.

"Look who Dana woke up." She giggles and her giggle is a bit above the level of a whisper. "Oops," she says in a very normal voice and she covers her mouth with her glass and hiccups.

This very awkward and charming moment makes me feel much, much more at ease. Holding Dana's hand had been 100% one of the most erotic experiences I'd ever had, which was saying something since I literally had sex with Kristy Lee like two hours earlier. Short, abbreviated, I-guess-we're-here, might-as-well do it sex, but still. But Melinda being silly and hiccuping and already breaking the whisper rule makes everything feel a lot more natural, more like a game and less like a secret suburban sex cult.

Next, Greg Supperville comes over and stands beside his wife and he leans across her to whisper in my ear, "Dressed up, huh?"

It's a weird experience, having a middle-aged insurance agent dude whispering in my ear but he smells fine, like cologne and red wine, and it's less awkward than I'd worried.

"Dana said it was ok," is the best I can come up with. I am kind of weaving close to and then back away from his ear, trying to find the right range.

"Dana can be very convincing," he agrees.

The party seems to be limited to the sitting room of their house, which is maybe twice as big as mine. It has two couches and two chairs and a fireplace and, most impressively, a wrought iron dry bar with a full wine rack and multiple types of whiskey and bitters and vermouths and so forth.

Dana whispers, "Can I make you a drink, Bob?" And I swear that either she kisses my ear when she says it, or potentially the B in Bob just forces her to spit a little bit. Either way it's super erotic and I can't even name any specific drinks at that point so I just nod.

Melinda puts her face between my face and Greg's face and says in a whisper loud enough we can both hear, "This is our first time at one of these. Thanks for inviting us, Greg. It's hilarious."

Greg nods and takes her by the arm and starts whispering things I can't hear. I aim for one of the couches, because Dana has left me a lot woozy.

Simon is across from me, on the opposite couch, just a little too far away to be heard. And his wife, Mindy, is sitting in his lap, whispering to him but he seems to be watching me, sizing me up, and it occurs to me that maybe I have upset the balance of the universe, that maybe cisgendered suburban whisper parties only work when there are equal numbers of boys and girls. But right now Simon is busy with his wife and Melinda is giggling as Greg whispers some nonstop stream of witty things into her pretty little ears and Dana is off mixing me a concoction that seems to be growing more and more toxic every second, and that leaves me and Jacob.

Jacob picks up his glass and lifts himself out of a chair to settle in next to me on the couch. At my party, he'd been wearing a t-shirt which was pretty stylish but still a t-shirt, but apparently he'd decided the Supperville's party required a little more class, because he is wearing some impossibly hip something, a concert tee for a band I've never heard of and a crushed velvet jacket just a little too small so it shows the gold watch hanging loosely on his wrist.

"Fucking weird, right?" he whispers.

And it is, but like Greg, Jacob feels preternaturally at ease in this situation, and maybe that's part of the key to his, Jacob's, success, he feels at ease almost everywhere he goes. And he smells great, a mix of floral scents, shampoo and wine. And I think, even in my straight dude/lizard brain, that I can totally understand why Kristy Lee fell for him the night of the Super Slaughter. And even as I am thinking this I feel Jacob's face not moving away from me. He is breathing in, smelling me and I must realize how completely I must smell like her, Kristy Lee McIllvinney. There's no way he could know it is her for sure though, is there? He must just smell the scent of a generic woman on me without any way to know this specific woman was once his princess, and still the love of his life? And yet Jacob is

189

still breathing in, letting the sex-scent coming off me fill his lungs and, once it has filled him up, looking away, and I can see only half his face then, and the half I can see looks like he is absolutely going to cry.

He steadies himself, takes a look down into his drink, takes a drink of said drink, a drink much longer than it probably has to be. And I keep waiting for him to make a juvenile locker room crack to mute the tension, something about me smelling like Tijuana or somebody's mom. But it never comes, either because Jacob is not the locker room type or because he recognizes somehow this scent, and it takes him back to a time he misses very, very much.

I feel like I need to say something to change the subject, which is weird because no subject has technically been raised. I settle on, "These parties always on weeknights?"

I am learning that when you whisper, you tend to use fewer words. It just happens naturally.

Jacob takes another drink and leans back into me. He doesn't turn his face to me, though, just angles his body so we are looking the same direction, which is across the coffee table at Simon and Mindy.

"Our first one. Hard getting a sitter," he whispers.

"I bet."

Dana has my drink ready. It looks like whiskey, but is several layers of syrup thicker than a whiskey drink should be. She hands it to me and as she does, leans all the way down to my level and I have to force myself not to look down her shirt.

Her face pressed between me and Jacob's cheeks, she whispers in both our ears at once. "I added truth serum, so he can't tell us lies any more." She winks at me and plops down on the couch next to Simon and Mindy. Mindy immediately leans over and starts whispering in her ear. I watch her lips move, try to understand what she is saying, but there's no way. Everything that gets said in here is heard only by the person and/or people it is said to. Not by anyone else. And certainly not by our phones, their 24/7 voice-activated virtual assistants always listening to us, recording us from our pockets.

Mindy slides off her husband's lap and onto Dana's and the two women very happily circle arms around each other's necks and start gossiping or trading stories or possibly flirting into each other's ears. Simon gets up with a bit of a grunt and after a stop at the dry bar, he comes over and sits down on the coffee table and since he is a big dude it creaks as he leans forward to whisper to me, his face on the outside of me and Jacob, so Jacob can't hear him at all.

"You got any investment tips for me?"

Simon's face is all faces. It is sometimes affable and dopey and it is sometimes loving and warm, but right now it is stoney and I can feel cold coming off his cheek. He leans back to look me in the eye and his cheeks are so expressionless they almost sag right down over his jowls. His eyes are the dead eyes of someone who believes 0% of what he hears.

"Ah," and I inexplicably choose to whisper the first thing that pops into my mind, "gold's a safe bet." And then I try to cover up, "And real estate," and I quickly realize how phenomenally dumb that sounds.

"You're paying for your house, investing in your house?"

Another thing I notice happens when you whisper is you can't really make hedging sounds like hm or um. You just slur your esses out into space. "It's other houses."

Simon is wearing normal-guy clothes while I am in my sweats and t-shirt and no shoes. Also I am barefoot while he is wearing boots with rubber soles and in the unwritten code of alpha males, this makes him a king and me a damn hippie.

Melinda and Greg come over and Melinda leans over Simon's back, so her face is right next to his face and the two of them appear to be some sort of two-faced monster. She whispers, "We were all whispering about you, Bob. This one," she points her finger down at Simon's head, "especially."

And they are all looking at me now, Melinda and Greg and Simon, all their faces right next to each other. And Dana and Mindy have stopped canoodling on the couch and both their faces have turned full in my direction. Only Jacob on my right seems to be looking away, awkward, bored, his brainspace still off somewhere else, somewhere not here. There is dead silence in the room and so I lean forward into its center and whisper to this sea of faces,

"Who wants to hear a joke?"

Melinda squeals, "Me first," and then covers her mouth with her fingers again and says, "oops" and "dammit, I did it again" in a completely normal voice.

I stand up and take her hand to lead her off to some other corner of the room. But as I go to stand, I feel Simon's palm on my forearm and it, his palm, is strong as bulls and cold as holiday sidewalks.

He puts his face so close to my ear I can actually feel his whiskers on my cheek as he whispers, "Real soon, I'm going to need you to show me that drinking game."

It takes a sec for the penny to drop and then I say, "Oh, you mean Chatt…"

But he claps his full, hard hand over my mouth so I can't breathe, much less talk and he says, "Shhh."

I jolt backwards, trying to get away from the hand but it follows me, pushing me back on the couch and for what seems like several thousand hours, me and him just look at each other, and the bigger my eyes get, the smaller his seem to be, his faceskin falling like a curtain from his hairline.

After a minute, mercy tugs on my arm.

"Come on, silly," Melinda Coral whispers. "My joke."

I shake myself free of Simon and me and Melinda go to the side of the room, where I tell her The Story of the Magic Frog. I take my time with it and we get closer and closer until we are standing with her chest against my ribs, close enough I can feel her skin stiffening as I whisper. But at the end, I have to be able to look directly into her eyes as

I deliver the punchline, it doesn't work otherwise. So I move only a few inches back and that means our lips are very close, almost kissing, when I finally say to her, "And that, your Honor, is how she got in my room that night."

Melinda jolts, electricity running through her body as she giggles. "Oh my god," she whispers, her mouth inches from mine, her tongue making little mouth sounds as she talks. "You're terrible."

I think she means terrible in that it, The Story of the Magic Frog, is a hilarious and dirty joke. She's smiling realistically, and her eyes are twinkling.

Mindy gets to hear the joke next, but by the time I make it to Dana, I am starting to worry about Kristy Lee. I am reaching my self-imposed one-hour limit, and that's what I tell Dana instead of my joke. She doesn't seem annoyed or offended. In fact, she seems authentically happy I came at all. She loops her hands around my neck and gives me a warm, friendly full-body hug, and whispers, "Thanks for playing along, Bob. You're fun."

I thank her for asking me over in the first place and wave goodnight to everyone but, on my way out, I put an arm around Jacob's shoulder and ask him a question that's been digging at me all night because of something Kristy Lee said.

I whisper in my good friend's ear, "Remember, a few days ago, you said something about the Super Slaughter. You said a bunch of accountants were in SuperMeme's books the next day. And I was wondering, that's Christmas

Day. So like, are you sure?"

Jacob leans back to me, starts to whisper, but then he rolls his eyes and ticks his head outside. "I'll walk you out."

And we head to the front porch, so Jacob can tell me a story in his normal voice.

Chapter 24
The Story of the Accountants

"The star was styled in the Canadian tuxedo, the blanket of blue, the all-denim-all-the-time look. And I had to hand it to the wardrobe department, the dude actually didn't look that bad. Somehow the ensemble worked and when the man walked through the doors of the diner to find the waitress smiling on the other side, their chemistry was undeniable. Sex appeal positively dripped off the two of them.

"'Now this,' I thought, 'is how you sell a pickup truck.'

"The director called cut and threw a look at me. I nodded. The director was a $10,000/day guy riding an Oscar he'd picked up as cinematographer on a movie he'd lensed for Syl DeMaille. What the hell was I going to say? Sometimes, you hire the right people and let them do their thing.

"I eased out of my chair in video village and walked back across the set to where the MOUNTAIN account lady was babysitting our client. 'How's it looking, Jacob?' she called brightly, knowing if I didn't want the client hassling me the rest of the shoot, there was only one answer I could give.

"I smiled, shook my head in mock awe, and popped a thumbs up. 'It looks beautiful. Just beautiful. That guy is a genius.'

"'What about the jean jacket?' the client asked. 'I was thinking, in the boards it was leather.'

"'Yeah,' I nodded. 'I had the same note, but the director asked me if he could try it and I have to admit, it looks really good on camera. Makes the color of the truck pop.'

"The first part of the sentence was a lie, I hadn't said a word. But the second half was true. And it seemed to satisfy the two ladies. They nodded and went back to talking about whatever marketing directors and account people discuss. Something important, no doubt.

"I wandered past them. The set had been built around an abandoned diner they'd found about 90 minutes east of Aspenroot on the 105. The day was coolish but sunny, which was a stroke of luck. A weather delay would've cost us 15% a day. Three days of that and the plug would've been pulled for sure. Then me and my producer would've had to go back East and tell the CD and the ECD both that they would be charging their client $135,000 for nothing.

That sort of pill could kill everybody's enthusiasm for the boards real quick, and make a reschedule darn unlikely.

"But none of that happened. I pulled off my sunglasses and squinted across dust at the highway a mile off. I could see motion. Maybe cars. Maybe trucks. Maybe just a mirage, a wavering of the horizon line.

"I walked over to a green and white striped tent pitched right at the edge of the set and walked inside. It was cool and shady in there. I was alone except for a craft service lady who was setting out snacks, and one of the film company's line producers who was watching her do it.

"The man was Australian, South African or potentially English. He had a bald head but was compensating for it fabulously, with drop crotch jeans and a beard that showed serious commitment. He smiled at me. 'So you're out here from Back East.'

"'I am.'

"'Answer me this. Why do Americans always call it Back East, even if they're from Kansas? It's never out east or east. It's Back East, like it's your mutual home.'

"I laughed at this charmingly accented human. 'Here's an even better riddle: why my agency's named MOUNTAIN. Offices in Charlotte, New York and Chicago. And it's named MOUNTAIN in all-caps letters.'

"The craft service lady'd laid out vegetables and hummus, which would likely be ignored. And a bowl of Peanut M&M's, which would likely be empty within an hour or two. The producer ignored the ladle and grabbed candies with his bare hand.

"'You got me, mate. But MOUNTAIN's a good one. I met some of your crew in Cannes last year.'

"'You went to Cannes? Oh, man, I so want to go.'

"'ECD and up, right?'

"I nodded. 'Couple more years till they spring for my plane ticket there.'

"'That's why they get paid the big bucks, mate. Where else you been?'

"'Around. I worked at the New York office of SuperMeme. We had an office out here a few years back. Sure you heard about that.'

"'Oh,' the producer looked at the ground. 'Horrible stuff. We shot with them, can't remember who.'

"'Oh yeah, what spot?'

"'It was a brand essence thing. A tech startup, an app, perhaps. Might've even been pitch work for all I know. Good people, though, smart creative team, good sorts all around. After the shooting, all our invoices were out and we were trying to figure out what to do to be a partner, not put you folks in a tight spot. Finance folks thought they'd call your boys in New York to offer an extension. But that day, that very day, we got a check for the sum of it, paid in full, accurate to the dime.'

"'Oh yeah?'

"'December 27, believe it. Someone at SuperMeme was on that ball.'

"I was surprised. 'Huh. That's cool of them. It was an

OK agency to work at. The New York and Aspenroot teams didn't cross-pollinate much. Kind of surprising you got paid out right, but it's good to hear. I only came out to this office that once.'

"And I rewound to Kristy Lee, the smell of Kristy Lee's hair, the feel of her hand against my lips, pushing at my face even as her legs pulled me in. I looked away to try to hide the red flush that accompanied some unnamed emotion I felt sure was crawling onto my face. 'Soon,' I thought and grabbed some candy for myself, just so I'd have something to hold onto.

"'Well, they did right by us. Guess they still have an office out here, though I heard they're down to just a few.'

"'Yeah, they moved into that Cash Register building.' Eyes still roving the floor of the craft service tent, I said, 'I'm gonna get back, see if the director wants another take or we're moving.'

"'Be with you in a minute. Cheers.'

"'Cheers to you, good sir,' I said to the producer with the beard and the drop crotch jeans I would see at the edit and most likely never again.

"I pulled back the tent flap and walked smack into the March sun."

"Somebody didn't want anyone to look into the books of SuperMeme/Aspenroot," I say. "Someone didn't want lawsuits and lawyers and accountants involved."

"Nobody should ever look at the books of any ad agency," Jacob says. "The world's on our ledgers.

Consumption is a drug and advertising is the pusher on the corner. That's all it is. That's what we do. We create addicts."

He polishes off his drink and heads back inside the Supperville's.

Chapter 25
Monsters

I wind my way home through our, me and Dana etc.'s, pretty suburban streets, made prettier by the darkness, the houses and trees all black-black relief against the navy black air.

My bare feet feel every bit of gravel that's ever been kicked loose from the asphalt and every speck of dust that wedges up between my toes. Who was I to ever have thought I could walk through this or any world without getting dirty?

I feel, in my pocket, the awkwardly large rectangle of my phone. I don't remember grabbing it on my way out my door. Then again, I also don't remember grabbing my keys or even really leaving my house to follow the mermaid song Dana Supperville sang.

I pull it, my phone, out by habit and it's still shut down from when I panicked earlier. I power it up and as the screen warms to life, my eyes adjust to its light, and that means that suddenly the neighborhood around me gets much darker. I am alone in a cone of blue digital glow.

I stop my journey, standing directly in the middle of some twisty street and stare as my phone spins up a hello message and pushes a notification that Webworld has automatically downloaded and installed Webworld WAR 2, the only app designed to control and sync with the upgraded Webworld We Are Recording 2 camera-based home monitoring system.

I look at this notification and know the answer to the question at last and I say this answer out loud.

"Chatterhat."

Somewhere, in the periphery of my vision, there is motion. My eyes flick to the side to see the front door of some stranger's house. No, not a stranger, exactly. It is the home of a family who receives, early Sunday mornings, from me, a carton of eggs, eggnog (but only once a month), a gallon of apple juice and a gallon of 2% milk. This house's porch's doorbell's WAR cam has flickered on. How do I know this? Perhaps there was a light that blinked? Or perhaps the lens, as it tilted in my direction, caught a bit of street lamp that then refracted off my eyes? I don't know, but I can feel it recording me.

Slowly I take a step and since my eyes are letting in so little light now, I can't see what precisely I am stepping into. It could be a broken bottle or a recently paved pothole or maybe I am about to stub my toe on a curb. I don't know. I just keep putting one foot in front of the other as I round the bend and see my house in the distance, just a few manicured lawns away and a few manicured lawns past that, on the street, the dark outline of the Crazy Suzy's Fish Stew truck.

I keep walking, basically blind, and all I know for sure is the name, the answer, and I say it again and louder this time.

"Chatterhat."

Suddenly the Crazy Suzy's Fish Stew truck seems to vibrate. It had been a silhouette out there, sitting on the suburban horizon. But now there is a distinct blue glow through the windows as if it's gone nuclear. Someone inside has flipped on a screen.

I stop where I am and I say the word one more time, and in this night in which no person is ever alone anymore, it basically sounds like I'm screaming when I call for the world to hear:

"Chatterhat."

My phone is clenched in my left hand, and my clenching is keeping the screen from going dark. I look down at it. I look up at the food truck. I look around at the menacing homes of all my friendly neighbors. I spin like a top, letting them all look back at me, see me alone and barefoot in their street.

I circle all the way around and around and then another half circle and then stop because on the street behind me, one hundred yards back the way I'd come, stands the monster.

He is so still he might as well have been rooted into the pavement, a thing that was never found only because it had never really been lost. Ten feet tall he is, maybe more, hulking shoulders and boney hooves, with two small horns ticking up at the moon from behind his ears. His fur is shaggy enough to blur his edges, so that I can not for sure see where he ends and the night begins. Even from where I stand, I can hear his ragged breath, a breath so large that every one he takes seems to expand him another six inches into the dark.

I stand on the street. He stands on the street. He is king of his domain.

The monster doesn't seem to be moving towards me or judging me. He is watching me, watching me like my neighbors and my phone and the whole world watches all of us. In a way, he seems less real than all those things, even though they are plastic and he is hair and muscle and horns and hooves.

He is impermanent. He is non-recording.

Still, I think perhaps it is best if I stop sharing this same night and street with him.

Very slowly I scooch my right foot sideways, sideways until I feel the asphalt turn to concrete. And then just as carefully I slide my left foot to meet it. I take the four inch step onto the curb and the monster does not care. He is a shape looming up the street, a monolith who seems to be ok with me exiting what's his, the night.

Carefully I sidestep my way up the path, up onto my porch, my soles feeling for the sidewalk and then the stairs, because I am absolutely not taking my eyes off him until I have unlocked my front door and gone into my home and locked myself safely inside.

The key is loud in the lock, springs snapping like branches breaking. I am holding my breath, and I am getting woozy but I worry if I let it out, what might that mean? Might he smell fear? Might he mark me all of a sudden, realize I'm prey?

I turn the handle and step one foot inside and then the other and then my hips and neck and last my eyes. But he, the Winegrove Goat Monster, never moves.

I close the door and am relieved and how insane is that? I, Dashain and Kristy Lee are no longer in any danger from the Goat Monster, because I own a home and it has walls sturdy enough to protect us from the very scariest physical thing the world ever whipped up. I can't get my head around it, it seems so fantastic, so glorious. All my held-in breath leaves my lungs at once and I collapse on the floor. My whole body, almost, goes limp.

My whole body except one hand.

Sitting there, on my floor, I realize that the knuckles of my left hand are not limp. They are the opposite of limp. They are tensed white and even starting to swell, my fingers clamping down hard on the edges of my glowing phone and suddenly all my fear comes back. All my fear comes back. All my fear comes back. My stomach starts to ache and the skin on my face starts to twitch as I let my eyes travel down my bicep, down my forearm, down into the white light of the screen.

I am now being pushed a different ad.

An ad for the Pwn It All pawn shop.

The headline says, "Sell everything."

Chapter 26
Pawns

The next morning I leave Kristy Lee, still sleeping, and Dashain, also still sleeping, in my bed and leave a new note on the counter, one which says I think I know how I can fix this for all of us, and she should keep my doors locked and her gun loaded and I'll be back soon and she should trust me.

Which I don't know why she would.

An hour later, I peek through the window of the Pwn It All pawn shop, the one I was in just a few days ago. The one I, apparently, had been to before and just forgot about.

There is a stereo in the window and where not long ago I would've imagined a sad dad hawking said stereo, saying, "I lost my job, got to buy my daughter a pizza for her ninth birthday, what will you give me for my stereo," now I think about some shifty dude missing teeth, beanie pulled low, surgical gloves on his hands so he doesn't leave fingerprints, spitting out, "Where'd I get it? Yo, it fell off a back of a truck. Whaddaya care?"

I need to see past it, the stereo, so I cup my eyes to the

glass and sure enough, Mr. She Say No Again is behind the counter.

I walk in casually, for I think the third time but like I've done it a thousand times before. I have my backpack on. I have a diamond in my pocket, a big diamond, and I'm casually keeping tabs on it with my fingers.

"Hey bud," I say. I am trying to appear shifty by trying to appear casual. But he does not say anything. He is looking down at a ledger he's holding in his meaty hands and then looking into the glass case beneath him and then he's looking at the floor.

"Hey," I say again, louder because I'm worried I am invisible again, maybe.

Standing behind me there is a shopper trying out a yo-yo. Who pawns a yo-yo? Don't they cost about $1 new? The yo-yo is going up and down, almost reaching something, and then pulling back, and then almost reaching it, and then pulling back, snapping back really, into a controlling hand which has the yo-yo's string looped around its middle finger so every time this prospective customer decides to send the yo-yo down to its almost-destination, he, the customer, is flipping off the world at the same time.

I try again, "Hey, got a minute?"

On a long table behind Mr. She Say No there is a model train set and it is looping not in a circle, but in a figure eight, going around and around in time, never getting anywhere. Every so often the train appears out of his right hip and then disappears and then appears out of his left hip.

Click clock clock. Click clock clock.

At last he slaps a leather square black pad on the counter between us and taps it.

I put the diamond on it. He bends down to judge.

"Seven thousand."

"This one's bigger than the one I sold you last week?"

He leans forward. "The more diamonds you have to sell, the less each one is worth."

"That doesn't make sense."

"It's the way the economy works. The supply goes up, the price drops."

"I don't think that's the same thing?"

"Listen, buddy, how many girls you planning to propose to?"

This is, in fact, exactly the reaction I wanted. I trace my finger around the diamond, making circles on the soft leather pad. "Let's say a lot. Let's say a guy had a lot. How would a guy keep track of all that cash?"

I pick up my finger. The soft leather pad must be gross as hell, because my fingertip is now practically black.

The guy says, "Go to a bank?"

"Maybe I need a," I say, "Chatterhat?"

The whirring behind me stops for a second. I turn around and the customer has stretched the yo yo string out wide. He is testing it for tautness. Is he going to run up behind me with it and strangle me? I look at him, he looks at me. He puts the yo yo on a glass dirty shelf and shoves his hands in his pockets.

I look back just in time to see the train appear briefly on the right side of the pawnbroker. Its clacking seems to be getting louder. It's almost deafening and maybe it's not just my imagination because the pawnbroker articulates, "What's that you said?"

I lean in, put one elbow on the counter, like we're two guys, just casually talking about a thing. "A Chatterhat."

He points up at the camera above him. He says, "Say it again."

There is a sign beneath the camera and it, the sign, reads, "You are being watched."

I say to the camera, "Chatterhat."

The pawnbroker shakes his head, like he's seen dumb asses like me before. "That's three times you said it."

"You, uh, you know this Chatterhat guy?"

"Who?"

"He ever wear a mask?"

"A what?"

"Like, a white mask with a smile? No? My bad, never mind."

The guy turns around and gets a stack of cash from a safe down on the floor. He slides it, the cash, my way. He says, "You don't want a receipt, I assume?"

"No but, so, this Chatterhat?"

"Just go."

Chapter 27
Coincidence

I am on the sidewalk shoving the stack into my backpack and it is lunchtime but I am still surprised when a (or maybe the) Crazy Suzy's Fish Stew truck happens to pull up next to me. I take a step and it starts rolling along beside me, smelling not like fish stew but the soot of a motor that has seen better decades. It seems to be driving directly on that fine double yellow line between conspiracy, coincidence and incoherence, but, all things considered and my head still a little sore in spots, I decide it's best to run.

My head decides this first and the sidewalk pitches at me dangerously and I realize that if my feet don't keep up, I'm going to fall on my face. Fortunately, they get the message and soon all of me is trucking - no pun intended - down the sidewalk. It's midday. It's midday in Aspenroot, one of the busiest cities in the world. And the citizens of Aspenroot are not happy with me running, mostly because all of them are looking at their phones and not looking where they are going until the last second, when they look up and say, "Watch it," or try to dodge me. But whatever they do, for just a split second, their phone is tilting up and the lens on the back of it is pointed at me.

"Quit recording me," I hear my voice yodel. It seems far away from me, behind me, as if my own voice is yelling at me and I am just a character I am watching on a TV show or something. "Quit recording him," I yell again and this somehow feels better, more appropriate. "It won't work anyway! He either is or used to be invisible!"

My backpack is banging into my back and so I take it off and wrap it tightly in my fists as I run, holding it up, trying to hide my face from all these phones. Why is everybody on the sidewalk on their phone? Why aren't we all running into each other all the time, every day, knocking each other over? I bounce into one guy and he's so into whatever is on his phone he doesn't even notice, he just pings off a store window and back into the flow of pedestrians without ever taking his eyes off his screen, like a fish that doesn't even feel all the rocks in the stream anymore.

Speaking of fish, now I am quite sure that the Crazy Suzy's Fish Stew food truck is after me because when I started trucking, it started trucking too and when it trucks, it really makes a racket, coughing and spitting like it has smoked too many cigarettes. It's pacing me down the sidewalk, but where I can dodge through people, it can't very well dodge cars. For a second, I think it gets stuck in traffic. For a second, I think I'm free. But then somehow it teleports in front of me, appearing at the next intersection.

I realize that food truck teleportation is unlikely, and it

is more likely that there are multiple Crazy Suzy's Fish Stew food trucks in Aspenroot. But damn, it looks like the exact same truck. I skid to a stop, first my head and then my feet and then my voice catches up from the rear, still hollering, "Stop looking at him."

I am out of options, with the crowd and the food trucks now bracketing me in, pushing me further away from the curb, closer and closer to the entrance of an alley from which I now hear a much quieter (than my yodeling) voice stage-whisper, "It's a government surveillance van, man."

I look into this dark alley and maybe ten yards deep there's a dark figure wrapped up in darker clothes, stringy hair a mop down over half a face, the other half not a face at all.

The alley is a vacuum, sucking in the air off the street and I feel caught in this flow suddenly. I step into the darkness and it's like I stepped into a refrigerator, the alley is so narrow and dark and cold. There's snow patches dirty in the corners and rats at work. The sun must never, ever reach in here, not even in Aspenroot, not even in the summer. And even the slightest noise echoes.

"You done something to attract the attention of the state."

Oh Simon, you son of a bitch, I think, as the half-faced man's echos bounce and soften and flatten and die. "Are you one of them? The feds?"

"No, I'm here because you said his name. Three times you said his name. And then some. In fact, recently you say it all the time, say it like you know him."

"Chatterhat?"

"See, there you done it again."

The half-faced man motions I should follow him deeper down the alley. At the end there is a metal door, and this metal door has a keyhole but no handle. Instead, the half-faced man sticks a key in the keyhole, turns it, and then uses the leverage of the key to pull open the door.

He waves me through, saying, "Go on, man. You said the name. It's time."

But me, I take a step back. I am thinking I'd rather take my chances with Simon & Co. than step into whatever lies beyond that metal door.

"It's time," the man repeats out of the good (functionally, that is) side of his mouth. "So you either come with me and get the answer you've been looking for. Or you don't, and maybe he decides I pay a visit to the blondie in your bed."

I go through the door and hear it close behind me.

Now we are in a long narrow corridor with a ceiling low enough I have to crouch to move forward. The concrete floor and walls are lit by single bulbs that have been strung out every 50 yards about, all connected by a long extension cord that must have been threaded through the tunnel way after it was built.

There are metal doors to our left and our right every 20 feet or so, and as we walk, they drift past, one after the next, drifting past like the promise of a strange hotel room.

None of them have handles, but every one has a keyhole.

"What is this place?"

"Aspenroot was built all of a sudden. And its barons and fathers weren't quite sure just how wet the winters might be. So as they built, they connected the skyscrapers each to each with these corridors. They run through almost the entire city. Fat cats would use them to make secret deals and attend secret parties. Whores would rush through them at nights like miners chasing news of gold. But today, only a few people even realize they exist, that everything's sewn together, it all connects back to the same place."

He slows to a stop and selects a door, inserts his key and pulls and in front of us, this dank little corridor opens into the light and the heat and the happy energy of the atrium of the Cash Register.

"Go on," he tells me.

It must be just the beginning of some lunchtime exodus, and people bounce by me, push on both my shoulders and I'm like a salmon trying to get upstream to spawn as I worry my uncertain way up to the information desk and her, the receptionist behind it.

She folds her arms and crosses her legs, leans back in her chair, all the power of the world for a moment concentrated in her having and me needing.

"Can I help you?" she asks.

"How are you, like, always here?"

"How much you want to know, Bob?"

There are many ways for me to take this. Like does she

mean, "What volume of information do you wish to possess?" Or, "What are you willing to do to find out?"

But there is only one thing that matters, which is that she knows my name, knew it before I even walked in, and while this isn't impossible in any meaningful sense of the term and maybe is even likely in a lot of ways, it still scares me, and it scares me even more that when I see that she sees it scares me, she smiles.

She tilts her head to one side and I see the half-faced man has crossed the entire atrium and is standing at the base of the escalator, waiting for me.

I go to him and the receptionist gets up and now she is following me. The three of us mount the escalator together, the half-faced man and then me and then the receptionist.

He leads us up, off, past the elevators, and at the entrance to the plush carpet hall, the pull of the air conditioning unit is very strong, even stronger than I remember, strong enough it almost, like, sucks me in and I feel like I am floating alongside the half-face man and the receptionist girl, the three of us being pulled deeper down the hallway, into darkness. Pretty soon, my eyes start to dilate but we may as well be in a cave, it's so dark. And then I see, way off in the distance, the size of a pinhole, the gleaming of the golden door. And it's suddenly so bright and my eyes are so wide I can barely see anything at all.

When we arrive, there is no key required, because there is no keyhole. The half-faced man opens the golden door, and we all file through it and he follows us in and snap, the latch and then another snap, a lock.

The room on the other side of the golden door is tiny, unpainted, like every person in the world just forgot it existed, forgot there was a room here that needed to be cleaned and painted and decorated just like any other room. The room holds one small metal desk with a calculator on it and behind it sits a man, pale faced and pudgy, melting into his chair. And I think I know his name.

"Joe Mead?"

"Indeed, indeed. I am Joe Mead."

"Chatterhat?"

"These days, but not always. But since you inquired, the original retired and offered me the mantle, should I be so inspired. But before we proceed, there's something I need you to know, and so I'll tell you so.

"There are three types of mysteries:

"The first suggests mysteries exist to be solved, they revolve around solitary sorts, strong and yet gentle, quiet but brave, the type of hero who's nobody's slave. And if this hero is dogged and stays the course, he'll work his way backwards to the mystery's source.

"The second type of mystery is a thornier thing, it plays like a song with no lyrics to sing. It avers that all mysteries are inherently unsolvable, that confusion is probable, and no matter how far the hero might go, the layers are denser than he can possibly know.

"And then there's the third type to which I must alert you, mysteries that doubt the existence of virtue. These mysteries could be solved, the facts are all there. But humans can't solve them because our minds are like air. Lacking purpose, devoid of imagination, dancing in the sun, chasing fascination. And if we do get lucky and stumble across a solution, we still won't recognize it for all the pollution. We chase answers not because we want to arrive, but because we crave a direction for our sad little lives.

"So tell me young Bob, once a robber named Rob, these are the types of mysteries three, and it's up to you to decide which one this should be."

All three of them stand there and look at me. Chatterhat is grinning from his chair. The receptionist, bored and wanting me to get on with it, cocks an eyebrow, which I assume would be difficult for the half-faced man to do, should he be so inclined. But I think only of Kristy Lee McIllvinney. And for some reason, I think about not her and me, but about her and Jacob Coral.

I think, and it's all I can think about, of a young woman giving herself to a moment, her mind and body one thing, and the way she allowed herself to be swept away while, floors beneath her feet, the slaughter of the century took life after life after life and a mystery was written, one which she never should have had to admit existed.

I say, "I want to know."

"Boring, but fine. We'll try to make it fun for you. Say, dearie, might you start us off?"

The girl had been snapping her gum and tapping her

toes and rapping her fingers, bored beyond belief, but now these three separate little explosions - the snap, tap, rap - become one rhythm, coalescing into a cool ragtime shuffle. And the half-faced man shoe-be-do-wops in the background. He's making words though, or maybe just rearranging letters, as he skitter-do-bops to the receptionist's time.

Hear chat.
Tar that.
Cheat her.
Eat cat.

Heart tart.
Heat chart.
Cart ear.
Reach art.

He char.
Each car.
Threat at.
Rat-a-tat.

Chat her at!
Chatterhat!

And Joe Mead sings.

Chapter 28
The Ballad of Chatterhat

Once a young lender realized he didn't matter.
That he could rant at derelicts, spitter and splatter.
And they'd mostly ignore him, no matter how much they owed.
No matter how many favors they'd taken and stowed.

But when he said he'd get his accountants involved,
The problem was almost always quite promptly solved.

So he decided he'd simply stop being a man.
And become an idea, and do the things ideas can.

He started a business with no story to tell.
He seduced his first customer with nothing to sell.
And when books didn't balance and phones started to ring.
He'd promise air or air promises, but never a thing.

One day, an investor said he wanted his shares.
So our idea shot him and scalped him of hair.
And then to make sure the concept took hold
He stripped his investor and cut off his nose.
Through the hole he pulled the man's brains, gray and runny.
And then he cut out his organs, his liver and tummy.
And he slopped them all in a shiny top hat.
And sent word to the street of his name...

[Sing it for me...]

If you had money derived from questionable ends
Chatterhat took it and returned dividends.
He took an idea economy that's not based on facts
And spun it into a place for crime lords to relax.

At SuperMeme, he'd bill clients a dollar for an idea sold.
But report one hundred times that, when taxes got told.
Out like a lord and in like a miser.
And no one who worked there was ever the wiser.
"We're getting paid what we're worth," they crowed to a few.
(Little did they know it was actually true!)

In advertising he found the perfect front for his lie.
Plus clients who pay and a license to spy.

You get hooked in for free to voice calls and data.
You can peek into inboxes and surveil the state-ah.

But one day a young innocent named Rowan McGregor
Made a quite honest mistake on the ledger.
She refunded a client the inflated amount.
The client returned the check and demanded a count.

Chatterhat thought he might take young miss Rowan
And hang her from a bridge with her arteries flowin'.
But a gory death might attract eyes 'pon SuperMeme.
The detectives might ponder, "Is this biz what it seems?"
So he hired me, a man without direction in life
To take Rowan to an alley and make quick work with my knife.
To state my real name surely I don't need.
But just in case, fill it in for me...

[Let me hear you...]

My first attempt failed, she threw her arm round my side
And took a quick pic for the whole Webworld wide.
I fretted my failure, grew nervous and tense.
And then the world went berserk by coincidence!
Some depressed looney went insane with a gun
And suddenly there was no murder left to be done.

Chatterhat chortled! Chatterhat crowed!

He thought I'd arranged it. His respect fairly glowed.
From that day on, I did whatever for fun.
And Chatterhat protected me as if I was his son.
A beef with the law vanished overnight.
A disagreeable dealer was crucified in plain sight.
And when Chatterhat decided to finally retire
He asked me if I'd like the keys to his empire.

I chortled! I crowed! I danced with glee.
Welcome to Chatterhat, an idea that's me!

It was my clients' diamonds you stole that night.
I've had spies on you since, to make sure I was right
And you weren't some threatening new robber quick.
You were just a young dumbshit, following his...

[Belt it out, now!]

But fate is stronger than previously suspected.
And my name you learned and my mystery inspected.
And so here we are, with our cards on the table.
Arriving at last at the end of my fable.

Chapter 29
Gunpowder

"So? How about it, Bob? Are you glad you asked?"

I shrug.

"Yep," Chatterhat/Joe sighs. "Well, I tried to make it entertaining."

"Hey, you did the best you could."

"It was the least I could do, since we're about to murder you."

"Wait, what?"

"All right. Now, we kill you now. Right, all?"

The receptionist had been sitting, one hip cocked onto Chatterhat/Joe's desk. Her finger snapping had stopped and her gum chewing and foot tapping had fallen out of rhythm and she'd begun to look vaguely disconnected from the whole scene. But now she is authentically engaged. She straightens up and kneels down in front of me and suddenly I am watching her pull a zip tie out of her purse. I realize what's happening and at the same time hands belonging, I assume, to the half-faced man are pushing down on my shoulders, trying to keep me in my chair. I jerk forward to escape him but the girl has one of my ankles in her hand and I trip, clonking my brain on Chatterhat's metal desk on my way to the floor.

The receptionist girl jumps on me, digs one boney knee into my back, and seems to be using it not just to pin me down but to actually cause me physical pain, grinding it playfully into my spine while the half-faced man finishes binding my ankles.

Chatterhat's voice comes from somewhere above. "The building should empty by eight or seven. So here's the thing we'll do to send him to heaven. We'll give him something to help him dream, and then take him to the basement where they can't hear him scream. A bat to the leg, a brick to the head, we'll beat him and beat him until he's quite dead. And then here's the twist and I don't want any shrugging. We'll dump his body behind Moo Cow and call it a mugging. But we'll leave a hat at the scene of the crime, with just a bit of his bits, to mark this murder mine!"

"Bummer, I liked Moo Cow," the girl pouts.

"We'll find you another job, dearie."

The man with half a face has a full syringe and he jams it in my arm.

I go to sleep and then wake up not like I have ever woken up before. Like it's the first time. I'm not really awake. I'm not really asleep. My ankles are still tied together but my hands are free because a tie on the wrists,

226

as I've learned recently, tends to leave a mark and these people, they don't want marks. Or maybe I am just easier to carry this way? I have one arm around the receptionist's shoulder and the other around the half-faced man's. One of them smells wonderful, like rosehip perfume. We're in a service elevator which is very loudly creaking its way the direction of down. Chatterhat the Second is behind us and he's this moment digging, in anticipation giggling. Dammit, now I'm doing it. Am I really this suggestible?

The door opens and the light from our service elevator spills into the basement of the Cash Register. It's exactly like that moment at a play when the curtains part and the spotlight shines. In this case we are the audience, and on the stage before us is not an empty basement, which is what I think we all expected, but a basement filled with wooden barrels. I have no way of knowing that these barrels aren't always here, of course, except that our elevator light has revealed one other thing. A man who is in the process of rolling one of these apparently heavy barrels across the floor. He stops to look at us and my captors stop back to look at him.

He is wearing the mask. The white mask. With the smile.

"What are you doing down here?" the receptionist girl says, in that sneery way that teenage girls have, even though at this moment in time I am 100% sure she is not a teenager.

The man, the Guy Fawkes fanboy, does not answer. He

lets the barrel rock gently in front of him as he turns his shoulders square to us and his white mask is the only thing that shines in this gray space full of mysterious brown barrels.

"What is all this shit?" she asks again.

And again he does not answer. But as if on cue, as if a maestro somewhere had tapped a baton, the masked man claps twice and then spreads his arms out wide, commanding our full attention.

He waves one arm down to draw our gazes to the barrel he'd been rolling. We follow, transfixed as he squats, grips its edges, and tilts the barrel back up so that it rocks solidly onto its base in front of him.

He knocks twice at its top and then raises one palm up to his ear and waits for a moment, but there is no answer. He shrugs helplessly, oh what to do? He strokes his mask-mustache for a moment and then, an idea occurs!

He leans down to the floor and picks up a crowbar. We gasp, but the mask smiles so beatifically! And so we relax as he prises open the lid to this one brown barrel. He stabs the crowbar inside and leaves it there, partially buried, as if it was a flag he'd planted to claim this soil in the name of some old forgotten king.

As one, we crane our necks to see over the rim of the barrel. Inside, there is a black substance the consistency of ash or rice or sand. Whatever it is, it is sparkling in this dim light, as if diamonds had been crushed and blended with charcoal.

He digs one gloved fist into the barrel, pulls it out, lifts it high and then opens it, allowing this mystery substance to sift through his fingers and waft back through the basement air, like the sands of an hourglass, counting down moments until the end.

The masked man nods knowingly at us, looping us in, making us realize that we are surely all on the same side, audience and performer working together.

He snaps the fingers of his left hand, ensuring we watch it as he again thrusts it into the barrel and scoops up a palmful of the substance, which, this time, he hurls directly at us.

And from his other hand, the one none of us had been watching, comes a match! And the powder pops and snaps, a thousand little fireworks exploding in midair. And he charges us through this cloud of sparkles and smoke, crowbar high in his hand.

He swings right to left and lands his first blow on the half-faced man's good side. I can hear the jaw cave.

"Oh shit," the girl says. She is trying to dump me but I loop both my hands around her neck, let my legs go weak, which they'd been wanting to do for a long time anyway, and drag her down to the floor with me. I start flopping my tied-up ankles, flopping like a seal, trying to kick the half-faced man in his now basically zero-face.

The girl is trying to squirm free. I roll her over on her side and grab her ponytail and now I start smacking her head into the concrete as hard as I can. It bounces the first time and then the second time her eyes roll and the third time there's not a crack so much as a splat, and her entire body goes limp beneath me. She's passed out. She's dead. I don't know. I go back to flipper-kicking the no-faced man.

Chatterhat/Joe and Guy Fawkes/Unknown Masked Man are circling each other. Guy Fawkes is smiling, at least on the outside. Chatterhat is giggling, singing, "Round and round and round we go. Death for one, rapture though! I'll take your mask, I'll cut your face. I'll wear your skin when I leave this place."

With this, Chatterhat lunges! Guy whirls, leaving a cyclone of black shadows in his wake and Chatterhat stumbles through them to faceplant into the barrel. He stands up and is slapping at his pudgy pink face like he's got a nest of bees on it, trying to knock the grains from his eyes when, like magic, a match appears in Guy Fawkes' hand.

He lights Chatterhat's face and a thousand sparks come whooshing forth.

He, Chatterhat, stumbles at me, his arms extended out like he just wants to lay by my side and give me the world's biggest hug.

And closing behind him, I can see Guy Fawkes rear up with the crowbar.

I shut my eyes so I don't have to see what happens next.

After a minute or more I open them. Chatterhat/Joe is lying on the ground in a pool of his own goo. Guy Fawkes is standing up above me, stroking his imperial beard, considering, pondering. At last, a solution occurs! He reaches inside his pocket and with a flourish, procures me a brownie.

"Seriously?"

He nods, white smile-face moving up and down, almost floating in the dark.

I open my mouth, a slave, and eat as I'm told.

Chapter 30
Home

I wake up, sitting on dewy morning grass, feet splayed out in front of me, on a greenbelt alongside one of those ever-so-straight suburban streets. I can feel a stone sign scraping against my back. I turn around and see it reads Winegrove.

I am home.

I drag myself onto my feet and stumble to my house because where else can I go? Where else would have me? I walk Winegrove's twisty sidewalks along fresh-cut grass and flowers in soft soil and wonder which, if any, WAR cams capture me as I drift to my front door.

Despite the fact it might be five in the morning, Dashain greets me in the entryway and I pick him up and scrub his ears to thank him for coming to tell me everything is ok inside. But instead of going in, I carry him onto the front porch and ease my way down onto my porch swing in the dark. He doesn't seem to care or be phased by a Great

232

Outdoors he has not seen since the day I got him from the shelter. He pushes his head at my belly and settles his ribs down into my thighs.

The view from my front porch is actually spectacular, if you think about it a certain way. A picket fence. Beyond the picket fence a sidewalk. Beyond the sidewalk a narrow street and then a suburban home that's pretty similar to mine in most ways. Walls that block the wind. A ceiling that protects you from the sky.

It's a surreal and sometimes gorgeous thing.

I wonder what Danica is doing, who she is doing it with, what her view of the world looks like and if anything is ever going to change it. Is she dancing? Is she in her bikini? It doesn't matter. She was too much for me, anyway, and that one big blinding piece of life she showed me was too much for me, too. Maybe that one night of stealing and sex took all the life I was ever supposed to have, used it all up, and now I'm meant to be just a particle, floating through the world.

Invisible.

Dashain is now snoring on my lap. I get out my phone, planning to check in on Danica, but then I remember my own little master monster plan:

1. Set up the tripod.
2. Hook my phone on it.
3. Hit record.
4. Leave Dashain alone on the deck.
5. See if a goat monster eats him, Dashain.

But I can't do it. Maybe because Dashain is my buddy now and he trusts me to keep him safe from goat monsters. And even if I could use my buddy like that, how much do I really want to share the answers to this mystery or any other mystery I may accidentally solve? How much do I want to define the surreal things that lurk at the edges of the suburbs, eating America's dreams one bite at a time?

I take Dashain back inside with me and I lock the door and go upstairs to find Kristy Lee asleep in my bed. I shower everything I can away and then climb in next to her and try to figure out what lie I can tell her about where I was all day yesterday, and also how I can tell her that it, whatever it is, is safely over.

A couple hours later, I wake up and Kristy Lee is making us eggs. The eggs are, of course, Moo Cow eggs. And the butter is Moo Cow butter. She is wearing a bra and panties in my kitchen and she is making us eggs. It's crazy. Maybe the craziest thing I have experienced in my entire life.

"You know Bob," she says as she scrambles the Moo Cow eggs in the Moo Cow butter, "this doesn't mean I'm your girlfriend."

I look at my phone so I can pretend I don't hear her. On that screen, now, there is major drama. Breaking news! Live video! Turn your volume on!

Kristy Lee swivels around to see what the racket is, which is this:

Last night, after the final no-collar creative genius left

the Cash Register building and after the final janitor had swept up the last crumb of the day and after the last security guard had jiggled the last lock, someone had detonated a bomb of some sort in the basement.

The building hadn't imploded into a pile of dust or anything. But the windows were gone, the golden facade had blown off the first three stories, car-sized sheets of metal and ungodly chunks of marble shooting outwards to litter the street. Inside, there was just dust, thick clouds that made it impossible to understand the extent of the damage. The main floor and the mezzanine had collapsed into the basement where, I knew, one day soon, they were going to discover the bodies of three people, pancake flat under all that rubble.

The lady with the microphone shouts at us through my phone.

"A Guy Fawkes mask, traditional sign of the anarchist movement, was painted on the street outside, along with the words, 'Ideas are worth more than we're willing to pay.'"

"What is it?" she, Kristy Lee, asks me.

Is this it? Has the revolution started?

The news reporter lady is stating there is a multimedia production company that owns a copyright on the Guy Fawkes mask but there's no word if they plan to sue the bomber for copyright infringement.

And also the display ad on the news site is now showing a selection of masks starting at $9.99, Guy Fawkes and otherwise. I start to swipe through them and then I realize how dumb that is. Now I am going to get served this same mask ad for the next week at least.

I say to Kristy Lee McIllvinney, "Probably not much."

I go to my front door to see some sun instead and open it, the front door, and here, in Winegrove, on this summer morning, the atmosphere is as gloriously still as ever.

Out on the street near my cul de sac, I can see the gray food truck parked. Except "Uncle Andy's Beef Bowls," it says on it, now.

On the sidewalk, here come Dana and Mindy, power walking in sun hats, both of them in red shirts printed with "SPIES are watching!"

And on every door a doorbell, and on every doorbell, coming soon, a Webworld WAR 2 cam.

Dana and Mindy give me a sunny wave as they pass my screen door and just as they turn the corner going one way down the sidewalk, I see a man about to disappear going the opposite direction. He's got his hood up. His hands are jammed in his pockets. He peeks furtively back over one shoulder like he thinks he's being followed and I see only half of Jacob Coral's false face.

I swing my door shut fast so he doesn't see me, and especially so he doesn't see the mostly naked woman cooking inside the four walls and under the one roof of my home.

Jacob walks on, walks away, passing through this early morning, a man waiting for the world to wake.

Chapter 31
Punchline

The riots never happened. The revolution was not Webworlded, except maybe in some dark corner, some message group where people like me ought not to go, because then we start getting served push notifications we'd rather not see and pretty soon we're watching videos about Martian surveillance and sovereign citizenship and, well, nevermind. If the detonation of the Cash Register building did anything to expose Aspenroot to the empty nature of consumer culture, everybody apparently took a peek and ran back inside their bubbles as fast as they could.

Late summer became early autumn.

I quit Moo Cow.

Kristy Lee got sabbatical and it was either a paid sabbatical or she was pretty unconcerned with it being unpaid or she was just used to being put on sabbatical.

I continued to pawn diamonds, but I couldn't quite bring myself to part with my gold.

I bought some runners and put them in my closet next to my sneakers, basketball and etc.

Kristy Lee, on occasion, came by my house. She and me would have sex and sleep late and get tacos and then watch TV with Dashain. Sometimes, we'd be talking about whatever and I'd ask her if she, instead of talking at a normal volume, could whisper whatever it was she wanted to say. She thought this was odd for about 10 seconds and then she couldn't get enough of it.

We had no future. It was pretty great.

One day, I'm lying on my floor, throwing my tennis ball into the corner between the wall and the ceiling, letting it trace an infinity symbol on its way back into my hand. In my pocket my phone vibrates to tell me I have a real live actual call.

I let the ball roll away on the floor and answer.

It is my dentist's office. They are reminding me I have an appointment later on that day. I tell them I can't go but they remind me that if I cancel I have to pay the cancellation fee but if I go, my insurance pays.

"So if I get my teeth cleaned it's free, but I have to pay not to?"

"That's the way it works."

"Damn," but I go. I don't have anything else urgent I have to do, right?

The dentist's office is super sterile. I am not sure how much of this is a front, just to put people's minds at ease. Is it really easier to sterilize the steel arm of a chair than it is to sterilize the plastic faux-wood arm of a chair? I am pondering this when the hygienist comes in and flips on that blinding light dentists use and positions it right in front of my face. Eventually, the hygienist appears on the other side of it, fingers hooked around a paper mask he is pulling up over his chin and mouth and mustache and nose. And my eyes are doing whatever the opposite of dilation is, to constrict, to limit, to allow in progressively less and less and less light. But I can not deny that I'm pretty sure I have met this man before.

"Your first name, it's John?"

"That's right." He snaps surgical gloves on his hands. "Have I worked on you before?"

"Must be," I lie, "that must be it."

The latex blue-gloved hands of John push their way inside my mouth, and he massages my mandibles and tugs on my tongue, checking for tumors and cancers and such. He hooks his fingers and stretches my cheeks open wide, first to the left, then to the right.

I close my eyes and I feel safe and warm at last, as the story I worked so hard to tear asunder starts, in tiny nonsense ways, to mend itself around me and the punchline becomes clear.

I smile and my smile turns into a laugh which hardens the O-edges of my lips. I try to stop, but it's not much use. I'm starting to cry, I'm laughing so hard. John slides saliva-slippery latex fingers out of my mouth and asks me what I'm laughing at and to him I say, "I got a joke for you."

Matt Ingwalson is the author of the gothic noir Mary Monster, *the award-winning revenge thriller* Sin Walks into the Desert, *etc.*

Made in the USA
Coppell, TX
08 August 2021

60172519R00142